PENTHOUSE PRINCE

Penthouse Prince

Virginia Nelson

Entangled Publishing, LLC
2614 South Timberline Road
Suite 109
Fort Collins, CO 80525
Visit our website at www.entangledpublishing.com.

Indulgence is an imprint of Entangled Publishing, LLC.

Edited by Stephen Morgan
Cover design by Heather Howland

ISBN 978-1507842430

Manufactured in the United States of America

First Edition February 2015

For my kids. Love you, my bratpack.

Chapter One

There were seven tan tiles and twelve white ones between the stalls and the door of the ladies' restroom. Jeanie Long counted them as she paced—*stomped*—back and forth and tried to calm her racing pulse.

She couldn't afford to be fired. In the time it would likely take to find a new position, she could lose the apartment. And her little girl Kaycee? She didn't want to think what would happen to her. Everything depended on Jeanie continuing to tread the fine line she'd so carefully managed to create over the years. To lose the job because of—

The facts of the matter steamed her temper to boiling. Her boss was a jerk, and someone should stop him. She'd known it for a long time, yet she hadn't taken action. If he managed to get her fired because he worried she'd tell someone she'd caught him having sex in the copy room, she'd risk losing everything. Normally, she could follow the chain of command and talk to his direct supervisor. But since the person she'd caught him screwing was his supervisor, she doubted the other woman would be receptive to her complaint.

Which left Jeanie little choice but to jump a few rungs.

Straight to the top.

She just had to hope that bypassing protocol in itself wouldn't get her fired.

She braced her hand on the cold tile wall of the bathroom. The motion set off the dispenser hanging there and washed her already sweaty palms in hot air, but she didn't care.

Camden James.

The press had dubbed him the Penthouse Prince, a playboy better suited to jetting around the globe and posing for pictures on sunny beaches than any actual work, but according to the rumors in her department, he was in house that week. She glanced at her cell phone and verified the time—noon. Lunch hour. Chances were good that he was sitting up there in some leather chair, and she'd be able to corner him—tell him what had happened and hope he'd listen.

Nothing left but to do it.

She snagged her coffee cup from the sink top and headed toward the bank of elevators reserved for the penthouse level. She'd never been up there before. Few who worked in her department had, but she might be able to find a way to make it up there. She did have her badge... It wasn't like the elevators only worked with a special key or code. Anyone could go up there, but you couldn't get past the front desk without legitimate business.

And she had the most legitimate business of her life. Her job might be on the line.

Perhaps she could just go up, talk to the boss, and everything would work out okay.

She stabbed the button with more enthusiasm than needed, and she cheered up a bit when she noticed a group of banker-looking types also waiting. If she got really lucky, one of them might be headed the same way and have clearance, and she could just trail after him—sneaking her way right to the top. The doors dinged, swished open, and she entered before the herd of banker types.

Gleaming brass reflected her tousled hair, and she lifted a hand to smooth it as music piped over invisible speakers and further grated on her already frayed nerves. The men smelled of too much cologne, and her destination… Well, if she actually managed to find the elusive Camden James, there was no guarantee he'd even listen to a peon like her.

She chugged coffee and stayed at the back of the elevator, hoping the suits in front of her would provide enough camouflage to get her to the penthouse. She never thought she'd see the big man upstairs in person, let alone talk to him, but what were her other options? Going back down and letting Derek fire her to cover his own bad dealings? Trying to find another job with benefits?

All the more reason. She'd rather get fired for trying. Which left her with nothing to lose.

A slight shift in the floor signaled they'd arrived, and the doors swished open. Her heart raced as she lifted her chin and pretended to be part of the group of bankers. She danced a fine line—too close to the men and they'd notice her and ask what she was doing. Lag too far behind the group and it might be obvious she wasn't with them.

What she didn't plan was being practically herded into

a board room. But before she realized what was happening, one of them was holding the door for her…and she had no choice but to go inside. She'd look even more out of place if she didn't enter.

The marbled floor, slick under her work heels, led into a conference room to the left. The men filed in and took seats. When a guy in front of her turned and caught sight of her, she smiled. His brows furrowed, as if trying to decide if he knew her, and she waved her hand at a chair.

A gentleman, he pulled it out obligingly, not questioning her since she still pretended she belonged. Apparently, she had him fooled.

Just act like you belong.

That strategy had gotten her out of some pretty bad jams. She hoped it would work this time.

Then all of the men snapped to attention. Anyone already sitting stood up, and everyone faced the doorway behind her. She froze. To command that sort of attention, just by entering the room, meant it must be him.

The boss.

She turned slowly, certain he'd call her out. She expected it, but she only needed a moment, long enough to tell him what was going on before he asked security to escort her downstairs—or off the property.

He probably wouldn't call the cops. It wasn't like she was causing trouble… She just wanted to talk to him. Supposedly, he knew all of his employees on sight. At least, that was what the last interview she'd read claimed. He might recognize her.

Even in her heels, she was eye-level with his chest. A steel gray shirt—his favorite color, according to the glossy articles printed about him—covered his expansive chest, the bland color only broken by his pink silk tie.

More a fuchsia? Maybe a hot pink? Crap, I'm panicking. Look up, Jeanie. Meet him square in the eyes and say what you came here to say.

She forced her chin up and took in his face, a familiar one since he graced more tabloids than the British royal family lately. He looked…

Tired? Yep. Mr. Bachelor of the Year, the Penthouse Prince, appeared exhausted.

She braced her hand on the table and waited for him to say something. For him to ask why she was in his boardroom…or assume she was with the bankers and speak to them.

At least, she'd intended to wait. Instead, the words blurted out of her in a rush she instantly regretted. "Wow, you look tired."

For a moment, a horribly long moment, only silence answered her. Then he spoke, his voice full of the same electrical charm that radiated from his television appearances.

"Darling, there you are. We've been looking for you."

What he'd said didn't register at first. It made so little sense that she just stood there, frozen, clutching her paper coffee cup and bracing a hand on the well-polished table. He closed a hand on her arm and leaned close as if to brush her cheek with a kiss. When his mouth was close enough to her ear that she could feel his warm breath, he whispered, "Play along. I'll make it worth it. We'll hash out the details later."

Breathless shock twined with confusion, and she allowed him to turn her, one hand steering her waist. She smelled his amazing scent, somehow sexy and male and blatantly expensive all in one, and that only added to her fluster. "I—"

He spoke over her and gestured to the steel-gray haired man who glared at them from the doorway. "Dad, I've not gotten the chance to introduce you to my fiancée."

Muscles locked in her legs, and she braced against his touch. "Sir—"

"Since her flight just came in, I'm sure you'll excuse us so she can freshen up, and we can catch up. Gentlemen, Dad?" Nodding to first the assembled bankers and then the man in the doorway, Camden led her out of the room and down the hall, his stride long enough that she was forced to race to keep up.

"Sir—"

"Shh…"

Did he just shush me?

"I don't—"

He pushed her into an office, closed the door, and then leaned on the handle, which left her to consider his back.

His most broad-shouldered and manly back.

Dah-um, the rich boy is built.

When he faced her, the exhaustion she'd noticed in her first impression magnified, and the cobalt of his eyes seemed brighter in comparison to the shadows almost bruising his face.

"We need to talk," he said.

She crossed her arms. This was her chance. "Yes, we do. I have a problem."

"Join the club, sweetheart. You may be the solution to mine."

What was he talking about? She couldn't worry about

that now. She might not have this chance again. "I work for you, and—"

"Perfect." He strode past her and riffled through papers on his desk. "I'm going to offer you a substantial raise, a new title, and a list of responsibilities to go with them."

"But you don't even know why I'm here."

He didn't seem to be paying attention to her. Instead, he slid behind the desk and began to tap out something on his computer. "Well, it doesn't really matter why you're here. You were in the right place at the right time, and therefore you are uniquely qualified for this position."

"Sir, I'm not sure what you're talking about, but I'm here about Derek, down in the call center?"

"What's your name?" He paused in his writing to consider her, *tsked*, and then tapped out more words.

"Jeanie, sir. Jeanie Long. I work down in the call center, and—"

"You don't work in the call center anymore, Jeanie Long. Like I said, you just got promoted."

"Sir, I think there might be some confusion as to why I'm here. I know, I probably shouldn't have snuck up here, no clearance or appointment and all that, but it's vital we discuss my boss, Derek. Aside from making some really ethically questionable relationship decisions, I have proof that he's skimming money. He claims he's buying lunch for us, and holding training, but in reality—"

Again, he brushed aside her words as if they were no more important than dust motes. "So, you're talking hundreds, maybe thousands of dollars, max? You snuck upstairs, invaded my conference room, to tell me about some small-time scam run by one of my employees?"

She bit her lip and nodded. This wasn't going according to plan at all. He didn't sound appropriately appalled.

She was going to get fired. This was a mistake. She never should have risked it.

"I'll fire him," he said.

"You have to understand, I had no choice but to—" Wait. Fire *him*? Not her?

"Now, moving on," he said. "Your job has responsibilities, as I said, that I think you might be uniquely qualified to fulfill. You faked your way up here—"

Oh shit.

"—I'm merely asking you to take part in another façade. The difference is that this one is worth considerably more money, will reap you far greater benefits, and will help me in the process."

So…she wasn't fired. And he really was offering her some sort of promotion.

"Sir?"

"A position has opened up in the company. You're going to take the job. In exchange, I'll fund a new wardrobe, expenses, pay you… You're from the call center, you said?" His fingers never slowed, flying across the keys.

"Yes, sir."

"So a grand a day would be a significant raise, yes?" Again, he pinned her with his cobalt gaze.

She swallowed. *A thousand dollars a day?* She could move out of her shitty apartment, put a little money back, get a new car…and that would only take a few weeks at that pay rate. *What kind of job is he referring to? That fiancée stuff…*

"Sir?" She managed the word past her suddenly dry

throat. "I work in the call center. I'm not a prostitute."

He couldn't be asking her to... She shook her head. It was ridiculous. But he'd introduced her... He couldn't possibly.

"I don't need a prostitute, I need a wife. Well, a fake one to replace my real fiancée who is shagging some actor in Cannes as we speak." One final sounding *click,* and he stood. He moved to a printer and pulled off the pages that it spit out before slapping them on the desk. "I wrote up a pretty standard gag order. Some of the perks I mentioned...and my expectations of the role you'll fulfill. Sadly, the duration of the position is unclear at this time, but I'll ensure you're financially compensated for the inconvenience at the time the contract expires." When she didn't move, he gestured towards the contract. "Sign here, initial each page." He tapped a pen on the stack.

"Sir—"

"Camden. If we're going to make this work, you're going to have to at least pretend to be comfortable with me." His engaging smile didn't lessen the weirdness of the situation.

"Camden, then. You're asking me to pretend to be your fiancée? Why?" The surreal nature of this whole thing slammed down on her, and she surreptitiously pinched her arm. Not even in her wildest dreams did she fantasize about the most eligible bachelor in America proposing to her—not to mention the unreality of the actual proposal.

"Not important. Sign the papers and get the job. It's really that simple. What have you got to lose?"

He didn't realize what he was offering. She'd come up here expecting to be fired, knowing it was her only chance to salvage her job. He didn't know about Kaycee, didn't know this could change their lives.

"You don't know me." She flipped through the pages and saw he was only asking for her to attend dinners or other events with him, show up at work upon occasion, and in exchange she got the money, a new wardrobe, a car… "I get to keep a new car?"

She could bank more of the money. Security, being in the black. For the first time, a glittering possibility.

Like winning the lottery.

But there has to be a catch.

"Yeah, you keep the car. I don't need another one." He picked the pen up and handed it to her. "Just sign."

"You don't know me," she repeated, and she put the pen back down. "You don't know anything about me other than I walked into your boardroom. How do you know anyone would even believe this? It takes more than clothes and a car to pretend to be engaged to you."

"I put that in. Page three. No sex, minimal physical contact, and only when it's needed to reinforce the illusion. I get it, not a prostitute, we went over that."

"You're rushing me." She flipped to the third page.

"I don't need to know you. You don't need to know me. It's a lie, a short-term lie, until I come up with another solution. You're perfect for the job. Just sign, we'll take you shopping and maybe get our picture taken…easy." He tried to force the pen on her again. Obviously, he wasn't used to people who didn't just blindly obey him.

She took the pen and pitched it across the room. "Not until you tell me the catch. What's this all about?"

He ran a hand through his hair and blew out a breath. "My father came for a visit. He's sick of my…God, my 'playboy ways' in his words. He still owns a large portion of shares in the company and threatened to make things a bit uncomfortable for me if I didn't settle down and get married. It's so old-school, but it's what he wants. I agreed…and upon me performing a double ring ceremony, he agreed to hand over his shares, making me the controlling shareholder."

"What about your real fiancée?"

He laughed, but there was no humor in the sound. "It'll be all over the news tomorrow. Suffice it to say, she's not my fiancée anymore. He met her, so that complicates this, but if I offer him a viable substitution and claim her story of our engagement was a farce, I can buy my lawyers a bit more time to find a loophole. Simple as that."

"Still not getting what the hitch is for me. Why are you rushing me? What don't you want me to think through? Like I said, you don't know me and—"

"I don't need to know you. We're not really getting engaged, it's fake. I need a female, and I'm offering you money to be that woman. Besides, my father will hate you. It's perfect." Seeming pleased with himself, he finally moved out of her personal space, which made her realize how much his presence jarred her nerves.

She wasn't sure what annoyed her more, how alpha he was, assuming he could get whatever he wanted…or how attractive she found him to be. "Why would your father hate me? You don't know a thing about me."

"I know you're sexy—though you could maybe use a day at the beauty spa—you're here, and your timing was perfect. Sign, please."

The cocky sonofabitch… It wasn't just that he assumed he was in any position to make this offer to her. It was that he assumed she'd so readily accept.

She'd had a lot of things assumed about her, and by people who mattered more than one egotistical rich kid. Oh, no, he didn't know her, nor did he even slightly comprehend how much one woman could rattle his chains, given a bit of time.

But the offer itself?

She would get much needed money, a car, a chance to knock an overconfident asshole down a peg or two, and then walk…taking everything per his own contract.

Yeah. It was a pretty damn good offer.

"Fine," she said. "Give me another pen."

"You gonna throw this one?"

She turned to leave.

"Hey! Hey, I was kidding. Here, use my pen. Maybe I should have written a clause about you having a sense of humor."

When she took the pen, it nearly slipped from her sweaty hands. The shake of her fingertips made her name look a little wobbly as she scribbled on the pages.

"Here, and here." Camden pointed, as if she couldn't see the lines that read, "Signature."

"Done." She turned to face him. "Not going to get down on one knee?"

His smile was fast and polished. "Darling, if I'm on my knees, I'm not going to be asking you favors. You'll be begging me."

She swallowed. He might have been riling her, but something about him caused her nipples to harden. She shook off the comment and set the pen down. "So, when do I start?"

The office door opened, and she caught a glimpse of his father waiting for them.

"Now," Camden said.

With that, he cupped her neck and took her lips.

Chapter Two

Camden understood the value of a gamble. Risk verses potential gain was math he calculated daily, and this wasn't any different. Seeing her, face pale with worry, one hand clenching a white and green paper coffee cup, the other pressed to the table, something in him had clicked, and the plan had snapped into view.

Pretend fiancée.

His father wanted him married. Faking it wasn't exactly a breakthrough idea. Since the sanctity of marriage was proven a farce a long, long time ago by his dad, who was Camden to break the mold?

Love? It didn't matter, and after seeing his father's example of a "loving" marriage, Camden had never believed in the fairy tale. He believed in dollars and sense, and money could make just about anyone see sense—or at least pretend in whichever way he wanted.

Which had everything to do with why he couldn't marry

his former fiancée, Tasha. Her failure to fulfill her role meant he needed to install someone else in her position and spin the breakup in his favor—fast.

His father just wanted the rings, and he wasn't picky about who Camden gave them to. After the way the press had framed his son—the Penthouse Prince, a playboy who'd sooner bring shame to the family than a wife and an heir—his father hoped that marriage would bring a sense of respectability back to his son and the family.

So what if it was an illusion? Illusions were Camden's specialty.

Seeing her, so out of place in the room full of suits, and having her notice he was tired when absolutely no one in his life seemed to see—or perhaps dared to mention—his exhaustion? Her instant of perceptiveness gave him a gut feeling, and he trusted his gut. After all, it'd always been right, even when his logical mind disagreed.

Her clothes screamed working class—a run in cheap nylons, uncomfortable, but functional. But her black heels. Hair fluffy with untamed curls. And her bottom lip…

He'd kill to taste her bottom lip just once.

But he knew what they'd agreed to. As much as he wanted to kiss her, touch her…he'd have to control himself.

He needed to get her agreement—preferably on paper that looked at least a little legal. The chances of her digging too deeply into the legalese were slim to none, but if she did… Nothing he could type up that fast would hold up in court for a minute.

But he'd been in a hurry. Enough that a quick agreement from her was all he needed. They could finalize their agreement later. Make it official. And legal.

Her questions had surprised him. Usually, if he threw enough money and perks at someone, they agreed without thinking it through. It made him feel a bit like the devil, signing deals which leaned heavily in his favor, painted with perks to blind his unwary competitors. But she'd seen right through him. He'd always ended up with women who fell for his games. What a shame that the one woman who might be his match was only his *fake* fiancée.

Now, as Camden pulled her in for a kiss, the shock on his father's face was priceless. The man was used to determining value at a glance, and he surely saw all that Camden did in this woman. Working class, average, not the fiancée of one of the richest men on this coast.

If not the country.

What surprised Camden was Jeanie's reaction.

Apparently quick enough on the uptake to realize she couldn't pull away or she'd blow his story, her hands lay only a little awkwardly on his chest, and her mouth gave under his. Her tempting bottom lip moved, and he couldn't resist a little nibble to test the feel of it.

The kiss felt more real from one breath to the next, and his hold on her tightened. The round firmness of her breasts pressed into his chest through her clothes, hard points signaling her reaction. When his tongue darted out, seeking entry, she opened her mouth, allowing the angle of the kiss to slant into something more.

Just the flavor of her was enough to leave his body hard and hot, tempting him to lengthen the embrace and enjoy the sweet nuances of her mouth.

His father cleared his throat, and Camden pulled back enough to meet her eyes. *Green.*

A verdant emerald, like the hills of Ireland, captured in her gaze.

He licked his lips and waited, expecting to see something on her face. Some sign of her feelings or her reaction to the kiss. But she didn't move.

He wasn't willing to release her entirely, not yet, so he pulled her forward. He leaned on his desk and placed her between his braced legs so he could twine his arms around her waist in the illusion of comfortable touching. "Dad? You didn't knock."

"Camden, could we have a moment alone?" His father adjusted his tie, his most obvious tell. He was pissed. So be it. He'd named the game. Camden only played it out.

"Sorry, Dad. Maybe later? Jeanie just got in, like I said, and I've missed her. We're headed out, maybe to do a little shopping and get some dinner. I'll contact Rachel, get her to cancel my appointments for the day. Didn't have much anyway, so I'm sure you can cover."

"Camden—" his father began, but the old man had spent years grooming his son for just this sort of situation.

Never let them get a word in. Keep them on edge. Don't let them see the chinks in your armor.

"Sorry, Dad, but I promised Jeanie. Maybe later? I'll call you, and you can come to dinner and get to know her, okay?" He caught her hand, spun her to his side, and led the way to the elevator. He pressed the button and didn't bother to look behind him. If he showed a moment of insecurity, the old man would swoop in and pick at it until he revealed the lie.

The doors opened, and he guided his new fiancée inside before he punched the button and gave his father a little wave. The moment the doors closed, he released her and slumped into the wall.

"So, you and your dad…not the best of relationships?" Her cool tone didn't reveal even a little of her response to his kiss.

It grated on his nerves that he couldn't tell what she thought. She couldn't have felt nothing. There was something there. Not that he should care, but…

"No, not the best. So, shopping sound okay to you? I can't guarantee the press won't get wind and come looking for us, but—I forgot to ask, do you have family or anything you need to let know about this whole thing? To keep them from spilling the proverbial beans and all that."

"None I can call, no."

"Should we stop and see them?" Suddenly more curious about her, he tried to see her face, but she hid under the veil of her now-loosened hair.

"I have a daughter," she blurted out. Those emerald eyes finally tilted up, and he gazed into them. "She's only five, though, so I doubt she'll pose a threat to your little lie."

"A kid?" *Shit.* A kid. "Are you married already? That would be a huge breach—"

He didn't expect the flat-handed slap to his chest or the fire in her gaze. "You really are arrogant, do you know that? If I were married, I wouldn't have signed a contract to pretend to be engaged to you. Who would do that? For money? Really?"

In his world, there weren't a lot people wouldn't do for money. "But you have a kid? Deadbeat dad or something?"

"Her father is not your concern. You signed the deal with me, not him." When the elevator opened to the parking garage, she turned away from him again.

"I may have signed the deal with you," he said, "but if there are people who might endanger the situation—"

"I can handle your lie. I have a kid, yes. You keep her out of this, though. Do you hear me? No one finds out about her. You're not fucking with my kid's mind just so you can screw your dad out of some shares in a stupid company."

She stomped away from him, and he waited, jiggling the keys in his hand. After a moment, she stopped, stomped her foot, and marched back to him.

"It's not a stupid company." He breathed slowly and held her gaze. "It's a multibillion dollar corporation."

"Whatever. Where's your car?"

He held his smile back with iron control. "It's *not* a stupid company. It's a very important company. The kid won't be a problem. I'll make sure she's taken care of for the duration."

She snorted and tapped her foot.

"My car is over there." He nodded in the direction of his Bugatti and watched as she walked away.

She had a nice ass, rounded.

Not that he should check it out. She was an employee.

Coincidentally, she was an employee he got to kiss.

They could pull this off. She had spunk.

"So, shopping?" He unlocked the car and slid behind the wheel.

"Works for me, Richie Rich." She leaned back in her seat and closed her eyes. "This day is officially the weirdest ever."

He laughed and glanced at his watch. "It's still lunchtime, Jeanie. Besides, I have the feeling this is going to get more interesting the better we get to know one another."

From seeing her and having the idea plop into his mind, fully formed, to her so near and intimate in the confines of his car, he realized he was having fun for the first time in a long time.

Not that he was going to tell her that.

Chapter Three

Shopping with a black credit card should have been a decadent pleasure, especially since Jeanie practiced budgeting more than splurging. But it was hard to enjoy herself when the card's owner loomed over her like some overzealous mother hen, approving or rejecting her selections.

She said, "Are you going to be this picky about everything? Because I don't think that was in your contract."

"You didn't read the whole contract. Never sign something you only skimmed, rule number one. That said…" He glanced up from the pile of purses the shopkeeper had collected for him and smiled a cockeyed grin. "It's rather amusing, actually. When I was a kid, I had dreams of becoming an artist. Color, balance…all of it fascinated me. It's amazing how much better we can make you look with softer fabrics and more vibrant color choices."

"Isn't it like putting lipstick on a pig?" She looked at herself in the mirror as she inserted the earrings he'd picked for this outfit. "I mean, because I'm in such desperate need for a day at the spa and all."

He came up behind her, closer than she'd expected. He seemed to do that a lot. The man really needed a lesson or two in boundaries, even if she had to admit it was nice to have a sexy man this close to her. She hadn't been on a date in God knew how long. Certainly hadn't kissed a man, and forget about anything else.

"Sure, you could fix yourself up a little. But I didn't say you're hideous."

She snorted—okay, the guy could make her laugh, she'd give him that—and spun so he could see the whole look. "Thanks for that. Not being hideous has always been an aspiration of mine."

"Not bad. So, the kid...why can't we discuss her?"

"Because it's none of your damned business." She slid back into the dressing room, pulled off the dress, and yanked back on her skirt.

"Come on, I'm curious."

She fought off a smile. "Obviously. You've asked ten times already. I'm not talking to you while I'm naked. Go away. Go buy some of this stuff or something. Buy the store. Just go away for a minute while you do it."

He wasn't charming, more of an ass, but his face... It never matched the whiplash of words. When he looked at her, he seemed almost hungry. Like he wanted to gobble her up in one fast bite. Then why had he made that crack about her not being "hideous?" Contradictions—he seemed full of them.

His low laugh from the other side of the door sent jitters of electricity skittering over her flesh. *Proceed with caution,*

Jeanie-girl. The man possessed a lethal dose of masculine confidence and oozed sensuality. His ease in touching her, his smile, his wit—all might prove a dangerous cocktail if she didn't remember exactly who and what he was.

She stuck her tongue out at herself in the mirror, and then she opened the door, only to find him leaning on the frame. "Ever heard of the concept of personal space?"

"Am I making you nervous?" He wiggled his eyebrows, as if they were flirting or something.

"No." *Liar.*

"Good. There's a photographer outside the window. How about a little love peck for the press?" His eyes, at this proximity, might still give the impression he needed a power nap or ten, but it didn't detract in the slightest from the raw power of his general hotness. He puckered up, quirked a brow, and she barely resisted laughing at him.

"Where?" She stood on her tiptoes and tried to peer over his shoulder.

"Look, kiss me or don't, but peeking over my shoulder might give away that we're aware of them."

She breathed out a gusty sigh, dropped back to flat feet, and placed a hand on his chest. "I'm just supposed to trust you?"

"In this case, yeah, let me lead. That'll work." He cupped her neck again, and she braced herself for the onslaught.

The man could kiss—she'd recognized his skill at making out in his office. He'd gone from casual to electric in less time than it took her to shudder out a sigh. So long as she remembered how fake both his kiss and his fiancé act were, she could do this.

This time, he paused, waiting for her to submit to his

touch, before ducking his head closer. Their breath mingled, and she recognized this would be different from his first fake smooch. He'd rushed before. Now, he took his time.

His lips on hers, smooth and cool, shouldn't have been so distracting, but she found herself relaxing into his light touch as he teased the corner of her mouth.

Acting. I'm just acting.

Yeah, right.

Keep telling yourself that, girl.

The feel of his shirt, soft under her fingertips, held the warmth of his skin beneath. A brief temptation to undo those buttons, rumple his rich boy façade, and slide her hand across his flesh tempted her while his mouth eased her lips open so his tongue could dance against her own.

Kissing a stranger shouldn't be this fun.

And in the kiss, it seemed the playboy faded away. Instead he was again the tired-eyed man who'd first approached her in the penthouse. The way he kissed her, it was almost as though he was asking her permission with his lips.

Was this another illusion?

But then his hand shook, just a little, when he changed the angle of her head. A catch of his breath, like he wanted her, and her heart raced in answer. She moved into his embrace, not sure if she was fighting for dominance or control…

The feel of the wall against her back awakened her from his touch, and she braced her hand against him. He stopped kissing her immediately, and she gestured at the door, unable to form words just yet.

He glanced back before shooting her a questioning look.

"The door. It swung closed. They can't see us. Wasted photo op." Proud her voice didn't quaver, she straightened her shirt.

"Yeah, well, me kissing you into the dressing room will make it look like I can't keep my hands to myself."

Is he breathless? Or am I projecting?

Since his fingers toyed with the ends of her shirt, as if he was about to tug it up and claim her flesh, she quirked a brow at him. "Apparently, you can't. Wanna back down, lover boy?"

He stepped away from her quickly, taking the warmth of his body with him. She fought down the urge to pull him back.

"Sorry about that." He smiled. "You know, fake kissing you isn't entirely horrible."

She snorted and snagged her purse. "Look, Romeo, you're really starting to turn my head with all these compliments. I'm shocked you're single, considering."

She'd intended the last as a jest, but his expression closed down, shutting her out. "Yep, shocker. Do you need an hour or two before dinner? You're going to have to tell me something about the kid, too, or I can't help you hide it."

"You really have to lay off that. I'm not telling you about my child. And, yeah, I could use an hour before dinner. You know, do the hair and makeup thing. Put on the fancy clothes, sharpen my talons."

He ran a hand through his dark, curly hair, and she envied his hand in a sick and twisted way. "I will send someone over to do the hair and makeup thing, as you so elegantly put it."

"I can do my own hair and makeup."

He scanned her, head to toe. "I'm sure you can. Probably. Maybe. Not that there's any evidence to support the supposition at this time, but who knows? You seem like a clever girl; you might pull it off. But if you're pretending to be my fiancée, you wouldn't have to, so I'll send someone over."

She shrugged. His money to waste. More money than brains—a catch phrase barely remembered from her grandmother—came to mind.

He pushed open the door to the dressing room—

And flashes from a camera going off blinded them.

He yanking the door closed and leaned on the wall. "Shit. Well, hmm."

"There really was a photographer." She didn't quite manage to hide the surprise in her tone.

"Of course there was. I told you, you can trust me." He pulled out a cell phone and made a call. He spoke fast, apparently his normal way, then hung up and dialed again. Within moments, the sounds of a scuffle filtered through the door, and he straightened away from the wall and held a hand out to her. "All clear."

"You managed to clear the shop with a phone call?" She followed him out of the dressing room.

"Two, but yes. Perks of being wealthy." He nodded and held out his business card to the shopkeeper, who looked a bit awed. "I want everything we selected sent to my penthouse immediately. Make sure it's freshly pressed and ready to wear, understand?"

A brisk nod and pleased smile was all the answer Camden got before he swept her out of the shop.

"You didn't pay for that stuff," she said.

"Another perk of being rich. They know where to find me. There are lots of perks to being rich. It almost makes up for the downfalls." He shoved a pair of sunglasses on his regal Roman nose and continued to tug her along. "Change of plans…you're staying with me."

"I can't stay with you!" She dug in her heels and locked her knees, grinding him to a halt. His brows popped up over the shades in askance, and her heart raced. She needed to get home to Kaycee, set up the neighbor to keep an eye on her for a few days, and try to figure out how to explain this mess to a five-year-old.

Someone holding a camera rushed down the sidewalk in their direction. Okay, time for her to get moving again.

Camden seemed to have the same idea. He didn't release his hold, kept their fingers twined together, and glided back into his power walk as if she'd never broken his stride. "See, we're going to have to talk about the kid. I mentioned that would happen. Actually, we should pick her up. Give me the address. Save me a Google search."

As he deposited her into the car, flashes of a distant camera caught her eye. She thumped her hand on the dash. "Dammit."

He slid into the driver's seat and popped the car in gear. "So where do we pick the kid up?"

"That's a terrible idea. I didn't agree to it."

"Would you rather the press discover the kid and get to it before we do? They're scrambling, as we speak, trying to figure out who you are, I'd bet money on it. How long do you think you have before they've solved the mystery and, because of you, find her?"

Like it would hurt him to lose a bet? The man probably bathed in money like that rich duck in the cartoon. However, he made a valid point. She couldn't let the press find Kaycee. If they picked too hard at that nugget of her past…

"Seventy-sixth and West."

He gunned it out of the parking spot, his smile only a little victorious.

"Doesn't this mess with your engagement story? Living in sin with your fake fiancée, now adding a kid they may or may not realize is hidden in your house? Wouldn't it be easier to back out now?"

"Nope. Hey, Dad wanted me to settle down, start a family. He probably didn't plan on me fast forwarding to the children bit before I got hitched but, hell, I've never done things the way he planned." In and out of traffic he slid, not bothering to glance her way.

She sighed and flopped back into the seat. "Maybe I should tell you a little about her. Just so you know what not to say, that sort of thing."

He nodded, and his eyes still didn't leave the road. "Deadbeat dad? I shouldn't mention him because it hurts the kid to realize Daddy doesn't care enough to pay his bit, see the kid, all that sob story stuff? Oh, wait, you got pregnant too young. He didn't want the kid, but you kept it? Now you're doing it all on your own, blah blah, cue the powerful yet moving soundtrack? I hear that happens a lot."

"No, Mr. Know-it-all. Her dad died serving our country in Afghanistan when she was only a baby. He was a hero."

His foot eased off the gas a bit, and he seemed to reconsider what he'd said.

"You're a widow," he said. "To a soldier. I'm so sorry."

She snorted. "You really must stop assuming."

"Tell me I'm wrong?" The challenge in his voice irked her. "I didn't nail any of it?"

"She's my sister. I've been raising her since our dad died.

So there, smart ass."

He hit the brakes hard, and they snapped forward against their seatbelts. She recovered herself, then realized he'd stopped the car and was staring at her.

Chapter Four

He tried to recover his calm, but she'd surprised him. *Again.*

The ability to throw him off balance made her unique. Few managed it. She was a damned saint. Who actually raised their sibling, called it their own kid, because their father died serving in the military? She was Lifetime Movie material.

People like that were snacks for the sharks that swam in his waters.

Yet she kept him on his toes, and he wasn't the least of his contemporaries. A glance shot her direction revealed her stealing a peek at her phone, her fingertip hovering as if she wanted to make a call, but she hesitated.

"So, your sister…?"

"Is a kid and doesn't remember our parents. I'm the mother she's always known, will always know. I'm her protector, and she needs kept out of this little lie. She's at an age where a father figure is something she's starting to notice the lack of in our household. We're not confusing her with this." She pocketed the phone and gazed out the window, still not looking at him.

He recognized it as her not giving him the whole story—more surprises for her to blindside him with later. He'd pick at it, figure it out before it became need-to-know information…

"We can set her up in my place," he said. "Hook her up with a nanny for the duration of your work, and you can be with her whenever we're in the suite. Not a problem. I'm sure I can hire—"

"If we're paying someone to keep an eye on her, I know who we're using. My neighbor. She doesn't work. She's on Social Security, has the time, and needs any bonus money she can pick up. You can hire her."

Finally, the flash of her eyes turned his way, and he identified a clear challenge in her green gaze. "Sounds like we're installing a few people. Guess it takes a village, in this case. Fine, we hire the neighbor. I'm assuming you can close the deal swiftly, get them both situated as easily? You know, so we can get back to my problems, the ones you're hired to help me solve?"

"Fine."

His phone rang over his speakers, and he flicked a button on the dash before answering. "Talk to me."

A familiar voice yelled, "Where in the hell are you? Stories are flooding the Internet—you're with some woman while Tasha is in Cannes with someone else—people are calling for a statement and I've got nothing. What harebrained scheme are you trying to pull, and why am I not in the loop?"

Lowe. Fuck.

As his best friend/lawyer/head of his public relations team, usually Lowe Richardson knew before Camden what irons he roasted on the fire.

Except today.

Today proved exceptional on many levels.

The snicker from his passenger reminded him to give only what information she needed to know rather than his usual brutal honesty. "I'm engaged, Lowe. The rumors are true, but the fiancée is an unknown who I've been seeing without alerting the media. Letting the world know today, shortly after my father had the great pleasure of making her acquaintance, was a tactical move on the part of our office because the wedding is coming soon. Handle it."

Camden reached forward to hang up, but Lowe spoke before he could disconnect. "Does the fake fiancée have a name, or are we keeping it under wraps for now?"

Good old Lowe.

The guy figured out fast where this was going. Quick on the uptake, earning the zeroes in his salary.

"Her name is Jeanie."

"Jeanie Long," the fake fiancée in question added.

"She's with you? Now? In the car, and you kept the call on speaker?" Doubt rippled over the car radio.

"Yes, we're off on an errand, and we'll be back in about an hour. Meet us at the office at my place. You can meet her. It will be swell." He flicked her another glance, then added for her benefit, "Lowe is my best friend, and you'll be seeing a lot of him over the next few days."

"Hi, Lowe," she muttered.

"Jeanie...so you're moving her into the penthouse? Do

you know her, or is this something we're playing out as we go?" It sounded like he was clacking at hyper speed on his computer.

"Just met. She's a great kisser; her wardrobe is being delivered, so someone should pick it up from downstairs and see that it gets put in the penthouse. I'm going to need a hairdresser and makeup person waiting for her, as well. We're playing it as we go, but we've got the details hammered out. Welcome to the party." His fiancée caught his attention as she gestured at a building, and he noticed her blush. He didn't comment on it, instead tamped down on his own little thrill at her reaction. Yes, his little employee could lock lips…but could she pull this act off?

He slid into a parking spot, then watched her get out and head into the building, not a single glance cast back his direction.

"She still there?" Lowe asked.

"Nope, just got out."

"What in the flying fuck are you trying to pull, here? Tell me she's not a hooker. I saw that movie, and it doesn't go that well in real life, I promise."

"She's not a hooker, she worked for me. Came up to my office, some complaint about her boss. Her timing was perfect. Dad was right behind me, and she played along until I could get her to sign a contract." He tapped his fingers on his steering wheel and resisted the urge to follow Jeanie—to see where she lived, what she used to surround herself daily. How a person filled her personal space said a lot about the person. Their nature, their likes…

"A contract?" He could hear Lowe smacking his hand into his forehead. "You typed up something, called it a contract, and now you've got some woman lying for you?"

"Pretty much. That's the synopsis version, anyway. Some photographers found us while I took her shopping. Gave them a little show. Dad's not buying this, but he's letting it play out. I think he's just waiting for me to flop this, so he can revoke the shares. I bought you time. Use it wisely."

He reached for the button again but stopped when Lowe spoke in a quiet tone. "You can't buy a wife, Camden."

"I just did. Meet me at the penthouse."

He hung up, then snagged his tablet and Googled her.

• • •

"A vacation?" Kaycee lit up. "Is there a hot tub? A zoo?"

Jeanie smiled and tucked a blond curl behind the child's ear. "Could be. I haven't been to the hotel yet. I promise, it will be very fancy. You can order whatever you want to eat. But I have to work, some, while we're on this vacation, so you're going to stay with Lori."

Wrinkling her nose, Kaycee bounced on her heels, which made tying her shoes all the harder. "Can I bring Mr. Lumpkins?"

Snagging the tattered bear, Jeanie then passed it to her before she glanced around the apartment. "Yeah, you can bring him."

If she were to take along something on this fiasco, what one item would bring her comfort?

Stroking a fingertip across a picture of their dad, she realized there wasn't a thing, not one little thing, she needed besides Kaycee. Her sister was the one remnant of their dad, of the illusion of family and security. The one fragment of

Jeanie's life from before it fell apart.

"Dad, I wish you were here. I'd love to hear your perspective on this whole mess."

"Are you talking to the pictures again?" Kaycee tugged at the end of her skirt then demanded, "I have to go potty. Take me first."

Complying, she waited for her to finish before closing the bathroom door and making sure all the lights were off. She didn't know when she'd be back home. This gamble might eat her life for a while, removing her from all she'd worked so hard to build and tossing her into a sea of the unfamiliar.

It would be worth it. Daddy had always said anything worth having required risk.

Pretending to get married? To a man like Camden? Risky. But maybe it was Kaycee's chance at a life like Jeanie wasn't able to provide on her own.

I'm engaged to one of the richest men in the world. Oh, shit, how am I going to pull this —

A knock at the door interrupted her racing thoughts, and she opened it to Lori.

"Hey," Jeanie said. "You ready to go?"

"As ready as I'm going to be. I packed three outfits, some pajamas, and some books. If this runs longer than three days, I'm going to need to come back here for more clothes and to water my plants." Lori looked calmer than Jeanie felt, her hair tucked back in a neat white ponytail and her soft face not marred by a single worry line.

"He says he's giving me a car. I'll give you a set of keys to it. That way, you can go where you want when you want. Just don't leave Kaycee. This whole thing is so weird. I don't want her alone without either you or me at all." She twisted the handle to the duffle full of toys for Kaycee and reached for the rolling suitcase full of clothes for her sister.

"Jeanie, look at me, girl."

The quiet words snapped her attention to Kaycee, who seemed oblivious to the adults, instead making a zooming noise with her one-eyed bear as she used it as an airplane. "Don't say anything, Lori."

The hand closed on her upper arm, and she breathed out a jagged sigh.

"Are you sure this is a good idea? You've worked so hard for so long, and this just seems…"

"Risky?" She accepted the hug from Lori before backing up to consider her kind face. "Yeah, this is risky and crazy and I don't know how I happened to be in the right place to get mixed up in it, but Derek would have fired me if I hadn't talked to Camden. His offer has nothing to do with me as a person and more to do with just being there when the opportunity presented itself. He doesn't know me. He doesn't want to. He wants to fool his father. If fooling the dad means I tuck back a few grand to buffer me looking for a new job, fine, great. Not to mention, he said he'd fire Derek. If he does, I might be able to get my job back in the call center when all of this is over and done, and we'll have a security blanket for a while. Whichever, it's more than I hoped for when I headed to work today. We roll with it. If, for some reason, they find out about Kaycee, though…" Panic swelled, a ball of worry she tried to swallow.

"What if you like him?"

The question shocked her past the fear. "Lori, I hardly think that's my biggest worry this week." Brushing aside the words with a wave of her hand, she grabbed the rolling bag and called to Kaycee. "Hey, kiddo, let's blow this Popsicle stand."

Bounding over to take their neighbor's hand, Kaycee beamed up at Lori. "We're going on vacation. I've heard of those. They're fun."

Lori sighed before returning her somber gaze to Jeanie. "You might like him. She's been your priority for so long, I don't know that you remember you're still young. Love's not impossible —"

Jeanie snorted. "This isn't a fairytale where the prince falls in love with the pauper and sweeps her off to his castle to rule over the evil stepmother. This is reality, where a really rich man who thinks he can buy anything bought some of my time because he's lying to his own father. Don't get your hopes up, okay? This is work, even if it's the weirdest job I've ever had. Nothing more."

The memory of his kiss, of his hand trembling, of how he smelled and how her heart raced, all of that might make her wish for a happy ever after, but she couldn't share that with Lori.

Camden James was a liar of the worst kind. Leopards didn't change their spots. *Liars are liars…and they stay liars.* Her mother taught her the hard lesson when she wasn't much older than Kaycee, reinforcing it a hundred times over.

It wasn't a lesson she would forget any time soon. No matter how great her Penthouse Prince might seem, it was pretend. She'd spent enough time with a five-year-old to know the difference between make-believe and the cold, hard reality of life.

Chapter Five

Closing the door to the rooms Camden assigned Lori and Kaycee for the duration of their stay on Easy Street, Jeanie took a bracing breath. Wandering down the hallway, she tried to remember which way led back to the living room and instead found the library.

Who in the hell has a library in their penthouse apartment?

Then again, who in the hell had an eight-bedroom home on top of the city?

Stroking the bindings of books, she jumped when a throat cleared. "Sorry, I—"

The man staring at her took her breath away. His high forehead softened by dark curls falling in an almost boyish charm drew her gaze to his startling gray eyes, lined by equally dark and heavy lashes. Model handsome, his smile reeked of charm. "I didn't mean to startle you. I'm guessing you're Jeanie."

Recognizing the voice, she tried to control her expression.

"Yes, you're Lowe?"

He nodded and closed the distance to capture her extended hand. "Yup, also known as the one person you don't have to fake it for. I'm curious how you wound up engaged to my best friend. Care to share the story?"

"No, she does not." Camden leaned on the doorframe. "Jeanie, I thought you'd get dressed. Makeup artist is waiting in your room with the hairdresser. All you have to do is sit, and they'll work their magic."

His tone didn't match his relaxed stance, and, if Jeanie didn't know better, she'd wager he sounded just a little jealous.

Ridiculous.

Retrieving her hand from Lowe, she gave an apologetic shrug. "Maybe some other time."

"Pleasure meeting you, Jeanie." Lowe seemed sincere, and she paused to consider him again.

Such a handsome and nice-seeming guy. If she'd met him under other circumstances, they might have become friends or… Knowing he was ass-deep in whatever Camden considered business took away from his appeal. "Likewise."

As she passed Camden, he snaked out a hand to capture her waist then leaned in close. "Hurry. My father will be here soon. He wants us to go to dinner with him. I'm still trying to wiggle out of it."

The touch of his hand sizzled heat right through her clothes, and she tried to shake off the reaction. "Will do, boss."

He released her, and she forced one foot in front of the other. One step at a time, the only way she could cope with all of this, she headed off to become the illusion.

. . .

Camden clenched the frame of the door, and Lowe poured a drink at the bar.

"She's beautiful," Lowe said. "You didn't mention that."

"You're right. I didn't."

Sleep. He really needed to get some sleep. Exhaustion left him jagged, oversensitive, like some walking exposed nerve. He wouldn't be bothered, if he wasn't so tired, at the tension in the room between his fake fiancée and his best friend. She was a pawn on the chessboard, and he was positioning her to pretend to be his queen—nothing more.

"She's attractive enough," he said. But he knew the truth. She wasn't beautiful in the stereotypical sense, not like the supermodels he normally dated. She wasn't just attractive *enough*. She was *more* than enough. His lips were still on fire from the last kiss they'd shared.

"Hmm…I can understand why you didn't mention it. A gorgeous woman like that, no wonder you felt she was right for the job."

Lowe didn't seem to notice a muscle twitched in Camden's jaw—a good thing since he didn't understand his response and couldn't explain it if his friend asked.

"I'm going to need your help to pull this off. Even if it doesn't last long, this is going to be tricky. Also, I need you to make sure the lawyers are working double time since I bought breathing room, but not much of it." He joined Lowe at the bar, then poured two fingers of whiskey and slung it back.

"Understood." Swirling his drink around, Lowe seemed

lost in thought.

"What? Say it. I can tell you're thinking something so hard, you're just bursting to say it."

"You like her."

Snorting, Camden slammed his glass back down on the polished wood a bit harder than he needed to. "Right place, right time. We discussed this."

"Any number of women might have fit the bill. You picked *her*."

Camden shrugged and paced the room. "I picked her, and now we work with it."

"You *picked* her."

Facing him, Camden risked eye contact. "So? I picked her."

"You've never picked any of the women of your life. Either they were handy, offered themselves up, or you knew they would piss off your father, so you dated them…or he picked them and you danced like a puppet. Her? You picked this one. You didn't have to jump at that moment, you could have planned this out better, but you didn't. That's a choice, even if it was a rash one." Lowe arched one brow, a characteristic expression. "I think it means something."

"Hardly." The denial tasted like a lie.

"Rumor has it your actual fiancée boarded a plane the minute the news of your new fiancée broke, heading back home. She hasn't released a statement yet."

"Waste of her time. I'm not going to meet with her while I've got Jeanie installed in this position. And I don't like Jeanie. I just met her." He realized going back to the topic would show vulnerability…moments after the words escaped.

"Ah, and it bugs you, liking her. Cam, I've known you far

too long for you to lie to me. Lie to the press, lie to your Dad, do what you have to do…but you can't bullshit a bullshitter." Lowe toasted him before swallowing the whiskey and placing his glass on the bar.

"I find her interesting." Admitting it hurt nothing, he rationalized. "She's not like anyone I've ever met, not so far. I'm sure it's just the puzzle. Once I figure her out, she'll become less interesting."

Lowe's laughter rang out. "Hey, man, whatever helps you sleep at night."

Nothing helped him sleep at night. Insomnia was his worst enemy. Not even Lowe knew that little truth. "I want you to stay away from her." The request surprised him, as did the vehemence in his tone, but he meant it, so he rounded on Lowe to fix him with a stare. "I mean that."

Adjusting his tie, Lowe smirked. "As long as she's your fiancée, I'll keep my distance."

Relief flooded Camden, but he refused to consider the whys of it right then.

Following Lowe out of the room, Camden breathed a little easier.

As Lowe stopped, waited, and finally turned, Camden recognized his expression and knew his relief would be short-lived before Lowe even spoke. "The minute you're split, though, she becomes fair game."

Camden didn't have a response, so he didn't answer.

The minute they split.

Eventually they would find a way out of this, and she would go on her way. But the thought of her then being with Lowe?

It shouldn't have made him jealous. But it did. And for the first time since this all started, he knew he was in trouble.

Chapter Six

The stranger reflected in the mirror frowned.

Pearls accented the little black dress Camden had picked out earlier, making her neck look somewhat swanlike. The whole getup reminded Jeanie of Audrey Hepburn... *You know, if Audrey had a curvy body.*

Snorting, she stuck her tongue out at the woman with the elegantly upswept hair and ruby red lips. "You still look working class, Jeanie-girl. Working class playing dress up."

Her reflection didn't have a rebuttal. She didn't want to like the makeover, wanted to be derisive of the clothes, but everything Camden picked had been clothes she might have loved to own, had she ever had the time or money to be concerned with that sort of thing.

The door behind her opened, and she pulled a neutral expression out of her arsenal. Seeing it was only Camden, she spun and faked a smile. "Well, dah-link, I'm all dressed up. This is my beautiful people impersonation. What do you think? Will I pass for the fiancée of the Penthouse Prince?"

"The tabloids gave me that ridiculous name. I'd love it if you could never bring it up again, thanks. And, yeah, you'll do. Did they fix your nails? Because they looked like a manicure wasn't something you'd even heard of." Stalking into the room, he seemed to take up too much space, shrinking everything around him with his sheer presence. His mood, almost lighthearted earlier, had darkened for some reason while she'd primped and applied her masking glamour.

"Nails, hair, the works. Is there anything I need to know before walking onto the stage, so to speak?"

He tilted his head, squinting as if considering the question. "We met at the office. You dumped a coffee on me in the elevator, our gazes locked, and it was history from there. Epic love story, blah blah blah. Oh, and I proposed at sunset. Yeah, that sounds pretty romantic. Women really get off on the death of a day."

She gnawed at her lip. "Very romantic. On one knee, I hope?" The rub of it was that it *did* sound romantic, but she couldn't admit that to him.

"Sure, but get all soft looking when you reminisce about it. After all, you're madly in love with me. Oh, and I'm going to be a touchy-feely guy."

Her eyes went wide. "Just how touchy-feely?"

"If I'm not, it won't look natural. Everyone knows how I am. If I reach over for your hand, take mine and don't flinch away. If I lean in for a kiss or to whisper, make sure you don't tense up. Just go with it. You probably know all this, body language one-oh-one from psych class or from your own experience about falling in love, but—"

Turning back to her reflection, she adjusted the skirt. "I've never taken psychology. You don't require a degree for hiring in the call center, in case you forgot. I had some college, but when I got Kaycee, I dropped out. And I've never been in love. Have you?"

"I'm not answering that." He dropped to sit on the bed, bouncing as if testing its softness. "But the answer should be obvious, since I mentioned I was engaged."

She faced him, considering what he'd said. Not answering meant he didn't want to. If the easy response would have been yes, because he was engaged, he wouldn't have added a caveat. "Wouldn't I know? I mean, as your fiancée, wouldn't you have told me?"

He surged to his feet and invaded her space. "Nope. Not my style. But I would have given you this."

He cracked open a blue velvet box and revealed a bed of white silk framing a sparkling, diamond-encrusted ring. Forgetting the conversation, she ran a fingertip across the ring. Lovely, probably worth a fortune, the band of white gold beckoned her.

"It's beautiful." Actually, she'd never seen anything like it. If she were to pick out her engagement ring…he'd nailed it. It would be the one in the box, hands down.

"Yeah, well, give me your hand. Let's see how well I did at the sizing."

Before she could offer it, he caught her suddenly numb palm in his own and slid the ring on her finger after tossing the box back toward the bed. "It fits," she whispered. *Perfect.* It fit and looked perfect.

He kept her captive by holding her fingertips. She couldn't lift her gaze, kept it locked on the shining thing as the air around her became too thick to breathe.

A gentle knock interrupted the moment and brought them both back to life.

"That would be Ruby. Dinner must be done. Shall we?" He offered his arm, and she twined her own with it. He began to escort her from the room.

"Are you sure this is going to work?"

His palm rested on the doorknob, but he froze, going statue-still. "The engagement? Fooling everyone? Or dinner, because it's not really challenging when you have a chef."

She licked her dry lips. "You don't think someone will see through it?"

He nudged her back into motion and positioned her against the still closed door, facing him. She studied his tie, trying hard not to inhale his intoxicating scent. "I think the key to selling a lie is to bathe it in half truths. I think, if we're comfortable enough together, if we smile and can't seem to stop looking at each other, we could sell it. Can you do that? Can you focus on me and only me, like I'm the thing that makes you get up in the morning and the last thing you think of before you fall asleep?"

Her breath seemed to come harshly, burning in her lungs. He was too close. His heat and body caged her in a cocoon of tension. She couldn't answer, her throat suddenly too dry.

He tilted her chin up, forced her gaze to meet his, and leaned close so their foreheads touched and his breath teased her flesh when he spoke. "Can you pretend to love me, even for a little while, Jeanie?"

"It's a two-way street." Her spine straightened, and she returned his challenge, cocked her head so their lips brushed with her words. "Can you pretend to love me, Camden? Act like I'm your sun and moon and you can't resist me? I know, challenging. I'm frumpy, after all."

His laugh shot electricity zinging through her blood stream and left her excited in a brittle way, like he could shatter the sensation with one wrong word. "You're playing a dangerous game, dear. I'm willing to bet I can pull off my end. Want to make a little wager?"

"I don't bet." She pulled back, impeded by the door, but gained a few precious inches of breathing room.

"Actually, I like the idea." His fingertip teased a trail down her cheek, then stopped after he stroked across her bottom lip. "Of course, if either of us fails, the other will cover it—keep the show going, so to speak. The challenge is to not be the one who requires a save. I'm willing to bet no one sees through me, doubts me, or questions my feelings for you. I'll bet you..."

He mulled it over while she tried to control her heartbeat, her breathing.

"I'll bet you this penthouse no one sees through my act."

She snorted. "So I can win this penthouse, on top of all of my pay and benefits, if I simply out lie you?"

"Yup. I bet I can convince the world I'm madly in love with you."

His tender look kept her off-balance, and she knew she couldn't beat him at his kind of game. He practiced lying, daily. *Seduction?* Easy for him. The tabloids told the story of his conquests—from actresses to one short fling with an actual princess—and they were many.

"What do you get? If I lose, I mean?"

He ducked his head, nibbling at her ear until she

shivered.

He is good—too good.

"What do you have that I want, little fiancée?"

The knock sounded, again, from the other side of the door, and Jeanie jumped, which put her in full contact with the length of him. She gasped, prepared to pull back, but he held her close. "I don't have anything you want. I don't have money, or things, or…"

"If I win, you'll marry me."

Her laugh broke free and snapped the tension, even though she still lounged in his embrace. "Yeah, okay."

"I'm serious." He looked serious.

She smacked his shoulder and scoffed, "That's stupid. Why would you want that?"

"I have to get married anyway. Why not make it a simple business arrangement? No nasty emotions to get in the way…it's perfect. I'm not sure why I didn't think of it eons ago." He seemed to be considering, almost weighing benefits against downfalls, while she watched.

"You want to bet on your marital status?"

He nodded, releasing her. He clicked his tongue. "Yeah, actually, I do."

"I—" She searched for reasons, ways to point out the stupidity of his plan. "Wait, unless you're so sure you can't possibly win?" It seemed ludicrous, but what other reason could he…"How would I even know you'd keep up your end of the deal?"

"Um, because I don't want to lose my house." He held his hand out and raised both brows. "So what you should be asking yourself right now is, 'Do I want to risk happily ever after with this man for a chance to winning the best real estate in the city?' If the answer is yeah, and you've got some balls about you, shake on it."

"But—"

"Don't think, Jeanie. Bet or don't bet, but don't waffle. It's unattractive."

She blew out a breath and clamped her hand in his. "It's a bet. I'm going to kick your ass, Camden James. I will out-love you, fair and square. Just do me one favor? Don't cry when you have to fork over your house." Her heart raced, and her palm broke out in sweat, but she didn't waver.

He jerked her hand once, his smile fast and more charming than he deserved. "Rule number one, little fiancée: never shake on a deal until you hash out the details. You didn't put any qualifiers on the marriage. This might be a mistake you later regret."

"Only if I lose…and I don't intend to lose."

"Let the games begin."

With that, he opened the door and graciously allowed her to pass.

And she wondered, for the second time that day, what in the hell she'd gotten herself into.

Chapter Seven

When he'd disagreed with Lowe earlier regarding the appeal of his hired date, he'd somehow convinced himself she wasn't beautiful. Striking seemed a more apt word, at least prior to her makeover.

After the makeover? He couldn't deny it—Jeanie wasn't just beautiful. She was gorgeous. Something about her filled his head with adjectives he'd never found apt in describing a woman before. Words like lovely, graceful, elegant, and mysterious. Not to mention sexy. Watching her from across the table, he wouldn't dream of denying his attraction. He'd not admit it to her or anyone else, but he could at least be honest with himself.

He didn't entirely believe his father got called away right as the help served dinner, but he didn't point it out to Jeanie. Instead, he leaned back in his chair, sipped a glass of water, and watched her revel in the meal.

Lowe left before dessert—a perfect tiramisu—landed

on the table, leaving Camden alone with the refined blonde who'd replaced the woman he'd hijacked into engagement. Without an audience, she visibly relaxed and dropped her act as if it were no more than a night wrap to be cast aside. Her casual comfort in his presence, after their short acquaintance, shocked him a bit. It might be another illusion, but he actually believed she might trust him.

Ironic, considering they were together perpetuating the biggest lie of his life.

But it felt good to be trusted. No one else trusted him, not even Lowe, and he was an old college buddy. Everyone knew what Camden could do and guarded themselves. Not that he blamed them.

She might not be high class, she might not be accustomed to the so-called finer things, but her pleasure in the meal and her ease of slipping into the role he gave her fascinated him. Almost as much as the speed she'd dropped it...

Licking her fork, her eyes rolled back and her cheeks flushed. He hardened, longing to shove the tablecloth and food onto the floor so he could yank her onto the polished mahogany tabletop and see if her reaction to him could match her response to coffee flavored dessert. The whiplash of desire left him shifting in his seat, tapping the table in conflicted confusion. One part of him wanted to satisfy his physical needs while the other reveled in the unfamiliar sensation of someone comfortable in his presence.

Conflicted. I'm never conflicted over anything.

"I can't believe you're not devouring this," she said. "Then again, you probably eat stuff like this at every meal. On silver platters, of course, with silver forks, all while pretending to be blasé when your chef serves heaven drenched chocolate confections." She waved the fork, eyes glittering with mirth, her sexy bottom lip pressed into a faux pout.

"Actually, I usually only pretend to be blasé when I'm eating off crystal. That whole silver bit? I think it's archaic, myself."

Her laughter bubbled out, surprising him with its unfettered joy. The curl of her red lips drew him further into her spell while the bright sound warmed something inside him, a piece of himself he thought long dead and buried. A twang of regret reverberated through him when she stifled her merriment to sip her wine. "I'm glad it's just you and me. For tonight, at least, I can enjoy the way the wine makes my head just a little fuzzy and eat like a pig. I think if I really was this disgustingly rich, I'd have a butt the size of Texas in a week. The food? Really amazing. Compliments to the chef."

"I'll pass along your compliments." With a flick of his fingers, he dismissed the wait staff. He'd do more than pass along the compliment. The chef would receive a hell of a bonus for impressing her tonight. He chose not to look too closely at his motivations, even as he leaned forward and steepled his fingertips.

"Thank you." He paused, considering his words carefully. "You did good today, really rolled with the punches. Not everyone would have followed my lead. Probably, it's going to get more complicated. We won't have a lot of moments like this." He wasn't sure why he felt like warning her, but his life wasn't conducive to private and stolen moments. He lived in a spotlight, part and parcel with who he was and what he planned to be.

She twisted her wine glass, some of her ease leeched away by his serious tone. "My dad used to say nothing worth having comes without risk. Do you think people are really going to buy this, though? I mean, you've upped the stakes with the bet."

"I think it could work." And that was true. He did.

He also calculated the wager before he'd gambled. She'd slip at some point. He could fix a small leak without a lot of work, spin being something he wielded without qualms. He wouldn't slip, not for a moment.

Pretending to be in love with her wasn't hard.

He might not believe in love, but he believed in attraction. He wanted her, regretted within hours his own hastily typed no-sex clause, and decided he would have her before the act was done. Sure, they'd agreed to no sex. But if she then agreed to renegotiate? If she decided she wanted him as much as he wanted her? Platonic business arrangement or not, he'd take her like he'd never taken a woman before.

He believed in planning. She'd make a perfect wife. No illusions about romance or need to win her affection—since he'd paid for her to fake adoration—would create balance and order where most relationships dwelled in a constant state of chaos.

He firmly believed marriage to be a social and economic arrangement. If both players understood their roles, it lowered the risk of unhappy surprises rising up and nipping the union in the ass. Her fierce devotion to her sister? Fantastic if he eventually decided to have children. She protected her sibling, so she'd be absolutely brutal in her defense of her own offspring.

If he'd written out a list of characteristics he desired in his bride, she'd earn checkmarks for every item he could think up.

She cleared her throat. "Sorry, woolgathering. Did you say something?"

"Just that I am probably going to head to bed, if that's okay. Or do you need me to dangle off your arm this evening?" Her smirk revealed her amusement.

"No, I don't need arm candy tonight. Thanks for asking, though." Polite. He wasn't doing too badly at staying polite.

Her snort, as she rose, contrasted with the elegance of her body wrapped in the black silk dress. "Fantastic. Do you have a game plan for tomorrow or is it more flying by the seats of our asses?"

"Flying, always flying. Planning isn't needed if you think fast enough." He didn't need to share his plans. She seemed to react well to impromptu, he didn't want to rock the boat and have her appear stilted as she tried to fit a scripted set of actions.

"Goodnight, then." She paused in the doorway, a sensual silhouette. Without looking back, she said, "Strange, isn't it? This morning, you were a stranger I'd only seen from a distance or in a magazine. Tonight, I'm going to sleep in your home with your ring on my finger after having you repeatedly shove your tongue down my throat. Life—it changes in a heartbeat, doesn't it?"

He chuckled. She had no idea. His life constantly changed at a rapid pace, leaving him scrabbling to catch up. He lifted his glass, toasting her back. "To more adventures tomorrow."

Her laugh trailed after her, elusive as the scent of her perfume lingering in the room and blending with the decadent aromas from their meal.

He glanced at the wall and toasted the woman in the large golden frame. "So, Mom, I think I met the future Mrs. James. She's not like you—she's stronger, more likely to not be destroyed by this family, but I think you'd like her."

His mother didn't answer, smiling eternally in dried oil paint, a ghost of the one person who'd ever loved him, monster that he was.

"She has a kid." He sipped the water, swirled the glass, listened to the chink of ice on crystal. "I need to find out more about the kid. There's something there, something she hasn't told me."

Secrets, in his world, never stayed secret. Someone would reveal the truth.

He just hoped Jeanie would be the one to reveal whatever she kept hidden rather than her past coming back to haunt her. He understood ghosts, believed in them more readily than the idea of love, and lived with his daily. After all, his father killed his mother as surely as if he'd wielded a weapon and taken her life. Ignoring her depression, practically being disgusted by her weakness—his father might not have killed her in a literal sense, but he'd betrayed her and been a deciding factor in her suicide. Camden wouldn't risk doing that to a woman.

Not when he knew he'd devoted his life to the company long ago. He would take the power from his father and then destroy the old man.

Another glance at his mother reaffirmed his resolve. He wouldn't rest—he'd promised her he wouldn't—until he avenged her.

Chapter Eight

Pinching the bridge of her nose, Jeanie resisted the wild and burning desire overwhelming her.

The stylist held out several different fabric swatches. "I'm leaning toward the reds. What do you think?"

Jeanie swallowed a gag as the motion sent another wave of the stylist's too-strong perfume rolling her direction. A headache wasn't just threatening at this point—it throbbed happily, right at home between her aching temples and blazing like a fiery sword behind her eyes.

If I look at one more piece of fabric, I'll scream, that's what I think.

Two days. She'd lived lifestyles of the rich and famous for two stinking days, earning every cent of the money Camden would pay her, per her contract. The time stretched out like her cheeks—which were sore from all the faked smiles.

"Stella, I think we've got all we need for now. You go ahead and order the things we've—" *And by we've, I mean you, since you don't actually care about my input.* "—chosen."

"Are you sure? We have—"

With a wave of her hand, Jeanie silenced her. "We're perfect."

Jeanie stood and escaped before the woman could follow her. Why Camden hired a stylist for a few days of faked engagement was beyond Jeanie, but she didn't question him.

Why bother? She was an employee. If he wanted her to sit with a stylist for an hour, she sat. Moments like the ones she just endured made her wish, if fleetingly, she actually planned to marry the man.

If she were his real bride-to-be, she'd give him a piece of her mind for hiring the over scented Frenchwoman to design her wardrobe. But she wasn't a real fiancée, so she stuck it out. Saved her bickering power for the arguments that mattered, rather than ones that didn't.

Seeing Lucas—the house elf, as she called him—Jeanie wiggled a finger. Actually in charge of the house staff, Lucas kept everything in Casa Rich Kid running smoothly. He also was a total sweetheart. "House elf, please tell me you can play Calgon and take me away?"

Lucas laughed and passed her a white plate. "I brought you some ibuprofen. You look like your head is hammering."

"Good eye, house elf. I love you, you darling man. Please tell me—" Before she could finish, he passed her a bottle of water. "My kingdom to you, sweet man. I'd give you a sock to set you free, but I'm not sure what I'd do without you."

Lucas leaned in to whisper, "Don't let the boss hear you, Miss Jeanie." He smirked. "I think he might get jealous, hearing you flirt with his gay-Jarvis-minus-the-motherboards."

Almost choking on the water, Jeanie laughed. "Where is my hubby to be? I haven't seen him around all morning."

"Uh." The tips of Lucas's ears turned red, a sure sign he wasn't allowed to tell her something.

She patted his shoulder, then swigged back more of the water, hoping the pills kicked in fast. "No worries, house elf. I'll find his lordship, my precious Penthouse Prince."

"He hates it when you call him that," Lucas warned her, taking the bottle back. "One might think you intentionally rile him at times."

"I'm starting to think I'm the only one who dares poke or rile his royal pain-in-the-assness." She shrugged and headed to her suite.

"You are. No one else would dare…" The words, soft and barely heard, made her turn to ask Lucas what he meant, or if she'd heard him right, but the man had disappeared.

"Oh, the secrets in this fancy house." Jeanie removed her shoes and let her bare feet sink into the carpet as she continued to her rooms. "We're not in Kansas, and I can click my heels together all day, but I couldn't make this museum a home." Not that she wouldn't put a damn good effort into trying if she won the bet, but still…

The highlight to her days were the moments she managed to escape her fake life and return to the real one. Kaycee kept her anchored, reminded her why she pretended to smile at all of the liars and snakes Camden kept around for reasons beyond her understanding. Reaching her room, she paused with one hand on the doorknob, as the child's laughter streamed through the closed door, embracing her in familiarity.

"What are you—?" Her words snapped off, killed an

early death by shock.

Kaycee twirled, her princess costume — topped off with a shining tiara — showcasing her little girl beauty. The sight of the laughing child, wearing what had to be a real tiara rather than a toy, might have been enough to surprise her — though in this house, maybe not.

She stepped forward into the room, but then she saw Camden, sleeves rolled up and shirt unbuttoned at the neck, sitting cross-legged in designer jeans on the carpet, with a pink and sparkling boa finishing off his ensemble, as he sipped from a tiny tea glass.

"Mommy!" Running full-throttle, Kaycee launched herself at Jeanie.

She dropped the heels — worth at least a week of her former paycheck — unceremoniously, scooped up the child, and rounded on Mr. About to be Dead Bachelor of the Year. "Why are you in here?"

"He visits me every day while you do assignments and learn how to be a princess," Kaycee answered, plucking at Jeanie's hair with her soft fingers.

"He visits. Every day?" Apparently, he had at least a tiny sense of self-preservation, because he stood, palms out in a peacekeeping gesture, while she closed the distance between them.

"Yes. He brings presents. I like him." The little girl squirmed, bored with affection. "Let me go find Mr. Lumpkins. He should come to tea."

Jeanie let Kaycee escape out of the room, then fisted her hands on her hips, one brow cocked. "You have all of three seconds to explain."

"I told you I was curious about the kid. You caused this.

Playing all mysterious about her wasn't smart. You've got to have figured out at least that much about me—just give me the information and satisfy my curiosity, and I'll leave it alone. So, really you should blame—"

She stabbed her finger into his chest, and he backed up. "Try again."

"Um, well, I like kids. They're simple, and this one is cute, so I just wanted to get to know her. Hey, I gave her a tiara, and every little girl should have her own tiara—"

This time, she smacked his chest with the flat of her palm…and tried to ignore how great his hard pecs felt under her hand. "Last shot."

"She's part of you, and I'm trying to figure you out." His gaze slanted away from her, and he twisted his lips into a fast grimace before shoving his fingers through his hair. "I didn't figure out any deep and meaningful answers about you, but I like her. She's sweet. And she calls me a handsome prince." He shrugged, a small smile ghosting across his lips while his eyes gleamed bloodshot cobalt. "What guy can resist a kid who thinks he's the hero in a fairytale? She also makes a killer cup of tea, especially for a child who hasn't been abroad."

The truth ringing in his answer relaxed her shoulders. "You've not let anything about her leak, right? No one figured out she's here still, right?" Panic might have reflected in her tone, but Camden didn't understand the shit storm looming if the world found out about Kaycee.

His brows snapped down. *Shit*. She'd made him more curious.

"No, no one knows she's here."

She breathed out in relief. Retreating might sometimes

be a noble move. She spun to escape him before he started picking at her like she was an interesting lab rat.

Passing Lori, who entered the room with a guilty look Jeanie filed away to ask about later, Jeanie called out, "I'll stop back in a little while, okay my Kaycee Princess?"

"Love you, Mommy!" The little girl didn't make another appearance, probably busy with five-year-old business, and Jeanie escaped the room.

She hadn't made it far, only partway down the hall, before his hand closed on her wrist, spinning her to face him. In one more move, he'd caged her against the wall.

"When are you going to tell me the big bad secret about your sister? I can't help you, can't fix it, if you won't tell me what's going on there. If this is going to work, honesty might be good, even if it's just between us."

The argument was becoming redundant; they'd circled this same topic so many times in the past two days without either giving up ground. On one hand, she wished she could just tell him and make it his problem. She'd carried the weight of it all so damned long that sharing the load would be a relief.

But the illusion couldn't become the reality. He wasn't an actual fiancé, he was a job.

"Camden, neither of us is being honest, so why try to use that? You're paying me to play a role, and I'm playing it." Usually, reminding him she wasn't anything but an employee with the weirdest job on the planet would be enough to back him down.

Apparently, two days of repeating this conversation didn't mean he couldn't change it up. "So, pretend with me. Pretend you can trust me. Tell me what it is that makes you get that hunted look, as if someone might hop out of the shadows and attack. I'm here for you." He stroked a lock of her hair, much as Jeanie might soothe Kaycee if she were upset. "Let me in, Jeanie."

She cleared her throat and blinked fast. If she shed a tear, if she let him know he got to her, he'd use the chink in her armor, and she'd forget where the lies ended and the reality started. "I got your email. So, there's a dance tonight and you want me in the green gown, correct?"

He sighed, sagging a little, looking a bit like a tired boy rather than a mogul man. She resisted the urge to comfort him, again fearing a slippery slope. He didn't sleep, not that she knew of, which explained his constant look of exhaustion. She'd seen him pacing last night and wondered what would happen if she went to him in the darkness. Would she see the mask of fast-talking, quick-witted businessman, or the softer one—the face she caught peeking out in moments like this one, when it seemed he let his guard down? Or would he be a whole other man, some stranger no one ever saw?

She didn't dare find out, so she backtracked, looking for an out from the intensity of his attention. "Camden?"

He blinked, the sleepy-eyed man vanishing in a heartbeat. "Yes, a ball for my fiancée. It's a benefit for the art museum, so wear that necklace I asked Lucas to deliver to you yesterday. We'll be doing dinner first. Meet me at the elevator by six."

Nodding, she waited. He'd still not released her. "Was there something else you needed, Camden?"

Ever the good employee, Jeanie. Remember, he's the boss.

A smile stretched his lips, gleaming white teeth flashed, and her sex clenched at the raw masculinity he could emanate with just a smirk. "Might be a few things on my want list, if you'd like to review it in my room." Waggling his brows, he grazed his fingertips up her arms. "We can still make dinner and the dance, promise. I'm good at multitasking."

Snorting, she refused to let him see what his constant refusal to respect her personal space, his scent, and their 'pretend' make out sessions did to her self-control. "Review them with one of your maids. I have a headache."

Not a lie, which he seemed to recognize, because he shifted, and his fingertips delved into her hair to massage her head. She concentrated on not melting into a puddle, but a moan escaped at the pleasure his hands brought to her aching scalp.

"Do you think having your hands on her every time I come to see you will make me believe you two aren't pulling something?" His father's voice hit her like a bucket of ice water, and she stiffened, even though she tried to stay relaxed. "You won't get the shares until you're married, son. How far are you willing to go with this farce?"

The tired version of Camden reappeared, and he rested his forehead on hers for a moment and whispered, "Gotta go. We'll talk later."

She nodded, and he dropped a kiss on her nose before moving down the hall to join his father and vanish into the study.

Legs gone weak, she allowed herself to slide down the wall until she sat with her face buried in her hands.

She could do this. She'd made it this far and she could keep up the act...but the text message she'd read with her coffee that morning meant time was running out fast.

I saw you on the TV. We need to make a new deal or I'm

coming for her.

She'd only read the words once, but they ran a repeating loop in her mind.

If only she could tell Camden. He could handle blackmail, probably win where Jeanie only managed to use stall tactic after tactic. Sadly, though, he wasn't her fiancé and couldn't be called upon to fix a family problem.

Her father, a hero, had taught her that family took care of family above all else.

For the first time since he'd died, she wished she could ignore his advice and just do what felt good—crumple into Camden's arms, enjoy wild monkeysex until she walked bowlegged, and leave the problems of Kaycee to...

But that was the crux. Kaycee didn't have anyone but Jeanie. Letting the wish go, like dandelion fluff on the wind, Jeanie forced herself to her feet to dress up for a ball.

Chapter Nine

Camden never drank heavily, preferring to keep his head and wits clear.

Except tonight. He wondered, gazing into the amber fluid in his tumbler, how much alcohol exactly it would take to wash her out of his mind, even for a while. Through the shifting fluid, she appeared, a wavering image in a gown as green as her eyes, spinning on the dance floor.

With a gulp, he emptied the glass and set it on the tray of a passing waiter. Long game, he understood. Planning, plotting, letting the pieces come into place before he made a move—none of that grated on his nerves normally.

Then again, he'd only known Jeanie for a few days. If he'd met her sooner, he felt quite certain she would have taught him the fine art of frustration long ago. Squinting, he forced his eyes to focus on the man who danced so expertly with his planned wife.

Lowe. Always Lowe. He should fire him. He could.

Chewing the inside of his cheek, he considered how hard Lowe would be to replace.

He sensed the figure approaching moments before the carefully modulated tone of her voice invaded his introspection. "I thought this whole thing was a farce, meant to hide the fact I cheated on you. Considering you're green with jealousy, I'm wondering if you strayed and weren't nearly as concerned about my indiscretions as I assumed."

Facing Tasha, he tilted his head and raised his brows. "I'd say it's a pleasure, but it's rude to lie."

"Always the clever retort, right, darling?" The champagne flute resembled the woman holding it—narrow, elegant, fragile looking. Long, jet black hair hung in a blanket of darkness around her tanned and sculpted shoulders, the silk of her skin enhanced by the ruby red of her gown. She looked up at him, her eyes so dark that they glittered like polished onyx.

His gaze swung away from her, seeking the vibrant light of Jeanie.

Tasha, not a fan of being ignored, leaned into his arm, and tendrils of her scent snaked around him. "Do you think she cares that you're gazing at her like some lost puppy dog while she glides in the arms of your best friend? Maybe she's figured out that Lowe is everything you can't possibly be— open, dashing, willing to risk his heart for the sake of love…" Trailing off, Tasha stroked his arm—petting him, really.

He should leave her side, go outside. Maybe get some air.

Instead, he contemplated her perfect cheekbones. "Love is a myth, and we both know that, so I have no clue why you're throwing that in my face. She's not like you, Tasha.

She's not like either of us."

"Hmm, you're rather attached, aren't you?"

"She's my fiancée."

"So was I, and I'm still wearing the ring to prove it." The hand wearing the band in question stroked his cheek, nails scraping lightly as Tasha's lips curled in a smile.

"So, hi, I'm Jeanie and who in the hell are you?"

He couldn't restrain a smile as he turned to his beloved pretend fiancé standing before them. He captured Tasha's wrist and regarded the curvy blonde turned fire-breathing dragon.

"Jeanie, Tasha. Tasha, Jeanie. There, now that we've done introductions—" He lifted a hand, signaling the waiter, who obediently supplied more whiskey. "Cheers."

He chugged it, reveled in the burn scraping its way down his throat, and waited for the wave of warmth to follow.

"We're going home," Jeanie stated, then turned to Lowe who—*bastard*—looked quite amused by the tableau of too many brides for only one groom. "Lowe, can you call a car around? He's not driving."

"Home?" Fighting to hold back a laugh, Camden reached for another drink. "Do you know where that is, little one?"

Jeanie didn't answer, and Tasha didn't back down. The idea of the two facing off didn't disturb him as it seemed it should, making him wonder if he'd drunk more of the whiskey than he'd realized. Scratching his cheek, he noticed numbness in his face, then wondered if his face or his hand had lost feeling. Maybe someone had poisoned him?

Tasha, dark hair a tumbling sea of night, stroked his arm, and he wondered if he should pull her closer or leave.

Jeanie decided it for him. Her fingers caught his and the little electric zing just touching her awakened seemed amplified at the contact. He turned to her and met her green gaze. "You look worried. Why do you look worried?"

"Aside from the fact I'm at a so-called ball with the handsome prince and he's shitfaced? And that I'm trying to think of a way to get you past the press without them seeing you hammered? No worries, Camden. I got this one."

He didn't resist the siren's call of her flesh, instead tangled his fingers in her hair and stroked her cheek. "This doesn't count for the bet."

She snorted. The inelegant sound, coming from her while she wore a green gown and her fiancée façade, cracked him up. "Oh, now he's laughing. C'mon, lover boy."

"You've not seen me really do my lover boy impersonation, little fiancée. Let me show you." His hand might not work right, but his lips did, seeking hers as they had repeatedly over the last few days. Her mouth answered his, demanding even as he tugged her closer. He trailed the kiss until he could capture her earlobe in his teeth, a move he'd learned caused the most delicious shudder to ripple through her temptingly curvy body, and he whispered, "I can show you so much, Jeanie. Let's pretend, just for a moment."

She didn't pull away, so he swept her into his arms, only slightly wobbling because of the warm fog of alcohol clouding his mind. "Oh, the press will love this," she whispered. "Especially if you drop me."

"I won't drop you. Let them take pictures. Princes are supposed to carry off maidens now and again. It's in all the books." The feel of her, all warmth and rounded curves in his arms, tempted him to move faster. Making it to the doors, cool air smacked into him like a wall, helping to clear some of the cobwebs.

The flash of photographers lit the way to the car, where Lowe stood by the door, a look of shocked horror clear on his normally impassive face. "Dear lord, Cam, how am I supposed to spin this one?"

Camden shrugged, not willing to release his armful. Instead, he sat her in the car, ignored her sigh as she dove for the waiting darkness, and clapped a hand on his best friend's shoulder. "Frankly, Lowe, I don't give a damn."

With that, and the sound of laughter rumbling out of the gathered crowd of media, he joined Jeanie in the car.

"Well, I don't know how you're going to explain this one, but I guess—"

He slid his hand back into her hair. He didn't want to talk to her. They'd talked for days. He wanted that full lower lip between his teeth, her arms around his neck, and he wasn't willing to wait to get home.

Frozen, she gazed up at him with her crystal green eyes, not revealing a thing about what she thought.

As usual.

"No one can see us, well, except the driver. What are you doing?" She whispered the words, as if she feared someone might overhear.

"For a second, let's pretend," he answered. Rubbing his nose against hers, he used his free hand to stroke the length of her arm, bared by the gown. "I need to see something."

"Camd—" He took her lips, silencing her. At first, she didn't move, simply allowing him to taste her lips. Patient, he tested her resolve, using nibbles he'd practiced for an audience.

Her fingertips, light as a butterfly, touched his cheek, and he leaned back enough to see her. "This is a horrible idea. If you weren't drunk —"

"Blame the drink. Imagine someone is watching. Whatever, just for a moment, pretend with me." He didn't know why it suddenly seemed so important, but he had to know. Had to feel.

Slanting his mouth across hers, he released all the pent up desire touching her wakened. He swallowed her soft cry and tried to fill the emptiness with the taste of her.

Chapter Ten

No girl dreams of Prince Charming getting hammered at a ball and carrying her off to a limo to try to make out. Even knowing that, she couldn't quite push him away. He asked her to pretend, but she didn't have to. He'd been seducing her since he swept her into a kiss in his office, constantly in her space, smelling like sin and tasting like—

Whiskey. He tasted like whiskey, and his brain probably fermented in the stuff. She couldn't take advantage of the fact the man had gotten sloshed, seen his ex…

"Wait."

He stopped, the pressure of her hand touching his chest enough to end the kiss. "You suck at pretend. I thought all kids learned this game?"

Choking out a laugh, she straightened his jacket, allowing herself a bit more leash than normal since he was blitzed and likely wouldn't remember. "I know seeing Tasha probably—"

"Tasha?" He looked genuinely confused, all tired man with tender eyes and no mogul Camden in his expression. "What does Tasha have to do with this?"

She rolled her eyes. The woman was stunning. Big boobs, tiny waist…if Barbie had a skinny Italian twin, Tasha would be that plastic figure. "Look, let's not lie about this. I'm not blind. She's beautiful. I'm—"

Normal. Not part of your world. From the call center.

Any number of answers died while he continued to give her his full azure regard.

"Not Tasha," she finished, realizing how lame the comparison was.

"I hadn't noticed."

She smacked him, which earned his lightning fast grin. "I think we both know what I meant."

"Look." He punctuated the word with a single kiss to the inside of her wrist. She tried, and failed, not to react. His seduction skills far outclassed her resistance ones, so the best she could do was to keep still. "I carried you out."

"Yes, well, although I appreciate your drunken caveman—"

"Stop talking." He licked slowly up her arm, then stopped at her elbow. "I'm telling you something important." He provided a slow lingering kiss at the bend of her arm, and she shuddered out a breath.

Keep still. Don't move.

"Okay." Her voice came out breathy, or maybe her heart beat so hard she couldn't hear right. Whichever.

"I know who you are, Jeanie." His nibbling mouth made it to her shoulder and she shivered.

Still mostly not moving.

His breath tickled her ear and her eyes slid closed. The scent of him, all raw man and wealth, went to her head, and she wondered, for a moment, if one could get contact-drunk.

"So will you please just relax for a single damned minute so I can figure something out?" She jerked away from him and saw his smile right before he unleashed a full tempest of need by taking her mouth in a way that didn't ask for permission.

He claimed her lips. *Claimed.*

Aw, the hell with it. I'm curious. What harm can a minute or two in his arms do?

The wet heat of his mouth demanded she answer his hunger, and she didn't have a problem coming up with a response. Somehow, her hand got lost in his hair, and then his fingers...

"Been wanting to do this." His whisper warned her before he slipped her breast free of the top of the gown and tweaked her nipple between his fingertips. The man had clever fingers, she realized, and then his mouth joined in his exploration.

She arched into the heat of his lips, and the dim light of the limo illuminated the sight of his head bowed to her breasts, those intense eyes closed as he sucked and she shuddered, a fist of desire slamming into her with the force of a Mack truck.

"Are we still pretending?" she managed.

"Yes, but I'm going to need you over here."

With that, he tugged her astride his lap, and her legs straddled his lean hips encased in dress slacks. "This might be going too far." But the sight of her skirt hiked up and his shirt rumpled where she'd tugged at it stole her voice.

His eyes, normally tired or inscrutable, no longer looked even slightly sleepy, even though he gazed at her from half lidded eyes. "We'll be home soon. Stolen moments, outside reality. We're still fine."

She couldn't argue, not when his hands streaked up her thighs to capture her waist, skin against skin. "Okay, a few minutes more can't—"

His lips found her again, tugged her into his embrace until she felt the hard ridge of him through his clothes. The sensation set off a firestorm inside her, and she gasped, but he swallowed the sound and mated their tongues.

She needed…something. Just a little more.

Unfamiliar tension coiled inside her, begged to be released from its tether. Unable to tell him, not having any words other than just telling him she'd never done anything like it before, she tried to think past the almost drugging passion he'd awakened.

It wasn't like she could just say she was a virgin—he'd laugh, drunk or not. Eyes closed, as if she could find control by not seeing him while his hands teased at her suddenly aching mound, she whispered, "I can't. I don't know how."

"You don't—" His hands stilled for a moment, then his fingers dug into her side. "Shit. Seriously?"

She didn't have an answer. The need sizzled away all coherent thought and replaced it with one drive. "Please," she managed, not altogether sure what she'd asked of him.

His thumb stroked her. "Trust me, just for a moment more, Jeanie."

She nodded, then sought his mouth and found it as he circled his thumb against her and made the coil of desire wind tighter rather than finding release. Then he moved faster, and his hips bumped into her as his finger thrummed at the wet, hot point of her need.

She arched her head away from him, then gasped as his mouth closed over her breast and drew it deep while he slipped a finger inside her. The touch seemed to fill a void, a hungry void, and she moved faster, driving her hips into his stroking hand. "That's it, baby. Let it happen."

A second finger joined the first, his thumb not slowing in its rhythm, and she cried out, the friction snapping her control like a rubber band stretched too far. Her thighs clenched, ripples of the wonderful feeling seeming to crest from the roots of her hair to the soles of her feet.

"Camden," she whispered.

He petted her through it, and soothing sounds and soft kisses brought her back from the edgy precipice. A warm glow seemed to bathe her whole body in satisfaction.

His arms wove around her and held her close to him while she tried to remember how to breathe.

"The car isn't moving," she finally whispered into his neck.

"Nope, it's not." Stroking her back, he shifted himself and sprawled a bit.

The hard ridge of him still pressed into her, and she fought a wave of embarrassment. "So, you're not going to remember this, right? Because you're drunk."

His snort echoed in the silence of the car. "Yeah, I wouldn't bet on that."

Not sure if she should pull away or what the proper etiquette was in this sort of situation, she chewed her lip. "Did you find out whatever it was you were trying to figure out?"

His laughter jiggled her on his chest, and she sat back, surprised when the motion caused a wave of new desire to waken. Trying to put everything back in her gown, he surprised her by brushing her hands away to help. "I found out more than I planned." He didn't look drunk, but she couldn't read his expression.

"This was pretend, you said so. I vote we just put it behind us."

He gently stroked her collarbone before he slid her off his lap and adjusted her skirt. "If that's what you have to do, Jeanie, feel free."

"But what about—?"

His fingertip touched her lip, and she met his gaze, still unreadable in the soft lighting of the limo. "Nothing in the world will make me give up this memory. Life is full of too much I don't care for, things I have to do whether I want to or not. The sight of you coming apart in my lap, your face as you lost all control with your lips swollen from my kiss? Not forgetting that. Shall I carry you in the house, or drop the knight with a raging hard-on routine for tonight, do you think?"

The cant of his head, the smirk, these expressions were more familiar and she breathed out, trying to rearrange her worldview. "Well, we're not doing this again, Camden. I'm not a prostitute."

His laugh trailed after him as he got out of the car and headed for the doors. She scrambled to follow him, one hand holding her skirt, the other trying to smooth her hair. He still hadn't answered her, so as the elevator doors closed, she rounded on him. "I said we aren't doing this again. It's not in my contract."

Not looking at her, he leaned on the wall of the elevator. "I'm working hard on control right now, and I did have a few drinks too many. It's not the best time to press your luck."

She smacked his chest, and he shocked her by capturing her wrist. The dangerous look on his face, sleepy moments before, should have scared her. Not turned her on.

One second she stood staring him down, the next he'd pinned her to the wall, pressing into her, his face too close. "I'm not promising we won't do that again." He arched his hips against her, the press of him shivering everything she felt in the car back to life in a heartbeat. "I will promise to be careful what I start."

She panted and the elevator dinged, warning they were at their floor and the doors would open in seconds. He released her slowly, the drag of his clothes against her body slow and sensual. "I—"

"Will *beg* me for more."

He stalked out of the elevator and vanished into the apartment, leaving her quaking, a little lost…and, God help her, desperate for more.

Chapter Eleven

Usually, the darkness held some peace. His insomnia used to bother him, but over the years, he'd come to terms with his nature and almost looked forward to the quiet hours of serenity. Few people stateside emailed him at night, his staff slept, and no cameras flashed. He could read or walk and plan without interruption. His complex life broke down to simplicity—one driving force—when he found time to be alone. *Avenge his mother, destroy his father, and control the company.* The trifecta of goals.

Tides were shifting, his single-minded goal blurred because of the path of distraction one woman carved in his sanity.

No peace came with the glitter of city lights out his window that night. His bride-to-be haunted him, probably lost in dreams in her room, with no clue he ached for her. He imagined her laughing with the wife of one of the board members at the dinner earlier that night and found no escape from his memories.

The woman got under his skin, with her potent blend of innocence and blazing sensuality, savvy chameleon abilities and fierce loyalty, beauty and brains. So many contradictions all housed in a body he longed to touch again.

The episode in the limo shouldn't have happened. If he'd said no to the whiskey, kept himself under control, he wouldn't have seen her—spine bowed in pleasure, golden curls falling like a treasure chest overturned, breasts heaving as she panted for him—and could pretend she wasn't more than an employee, hired to serve a purpose.

He might not be wondering what it would be like to take her on a bed, a table, bent over a couch, her deliciously responsive body shivering with passion as she cried out.

He could pretend he didn't remember the feel of her, legs spread, hips pistoning into his hand as she shattered, leaving him in a thousand pieces he longed for her to assemble. He might even be able to forget her latest surprise.

A virgin. *Who, in this day and age, makes it to their late twenties with their purity intact?*

His bride-to-be, that's who.

It made sense, when he considered her explanation of her life, piecemeal as it might have been. She'd given up everything when her father died, for the kid, Kaycee. Sacrificing her own education, dreams—*what were her dreams?*—and life, she'd become a mother to her sibling. From his time with the child, he could see she'd done a good job as an impromptu parent. Kaycee had bloomed, a funny and smart kid with a contagious belly laugh, secure in her world and oblivious to the fact her sister lived a lie for that security.

It didn't explain how she'd made it into college and kept her virginity. The woman oozed sexual grace, gowned earlier that evening in a low-backed dress which drew attention to the curve of her rounded hips, the delicacy of her spine, the elegance of her posture. How could the woman he pretended to adore be untouched?

No one in the room would believe it if she claimed it. But in her helpless plea, her unrestrained and desperate submission to his touch, she'd revealed more in those stolen moments than in all of the arguments or conversations they'd shared to date.

Knowing it should have made her less desirable— *Who wanted to try to train a virgin how to fuck? Who had time for that?* Awkward sex was for teenage years, for fumbling and groping when your hormones were untamed enough not to care about clacking teeth and breaking hymens.

But the knowledge didn't stop him from having barbarian-variety thoughts about teaching her how to make love, of showing her the world of carnal pleasure one tasty nugget at a time and watching her come to terms with her very sexual nature.

A soft knock disturbed his reverie, and he turned to see her peeking in. "Hey," she whispered.

Turning back to his study of the city, he wished she hadn't come to him—not at night. He didn't like to pretend when darkness should shroud him from public consumption. "You should get some sleep. It's late." He didn't attempt to keep the harsh command out of his tone.

The soft whisper of fabric alerted him to her disregard of his advice and his body, attuned to her, vibrated like someone twanged a string deep inside him in response to the delicate scent of her shampoo.

"I can't sleep. Neither can you, obviously. When do you sleep? When I get up in the morning, you're already dressed and going. When I turn in at night, you're still up. Do you ever sleep, rich kid?" Her voice, pitched low in deference to the sleeping household, seemed intimate somehow.

"I prefer to be alone at night. Your services are not required. The library is extensive, however, and you're welcome to find a book of your choosing." *Distance.* If he kept his distance, she might not realize he couldn't stop thinking about her, wondering at the mysteries she refused to reveal.

"Well, sir high and mighty, you can play lord of the manor with any number of your employees, but it doesn't work with me. You can't shove your tongue down my throat all day long and hide behind your mask at home. It just doesn't work like that." He turned to see her, legs folded under her in a soft chair, green gaze turned to the view out the bay windows. "It's pretty in here at night. I can see why you'd choose this for your lair."

He chuckled and scrubbed his hands across his face. Exhaustion tugged at him, teasing him with the prospect of sleep he knew would elude him. "Lair? You make me sound like some evil villain from a comic book."

She tilted her head. Her night robe parted just enough for him to glimpse, in the barely lit room, the peaches and cream of her flesh under silk. "Aren't you? Plotting and scheming, trying to take over the world. But when do you rest, Camden?"

He didn't have answers, and she'd invaded his space, so he returned the gesture, lifting her and settling her into his lap. Warm, sweet smelling, her tiny gasp curled his lips up in a smile. "No rest for the wicked, sweetheart. Surely you've heard that one."

She didn't resist him, never resisted him, instead relaxed into his arms as if she belonged there. "Are you wicked, Penthouse Prince?" Her head rested on his shoulder and snuggled him as if they'd been married for years, and she was simply seeking respite from bad dreams.

His body reacted to her—he always responded to her, regardless of the situation—but he smoothed her hair before rubbing slow circles on her back until she sighed. "Sometimes I think I am."

Burrowing deeper into his embrace, her breathing slowed. He wondered if she could fall asleep with him, trust him that much, and suddenly wanted her to. Encouraging her to relax further, he sprawled out his legs and rested his head against hers so he could feel her breath feather his face.

"I don't think you're evil, prince charming with a credit card. I wish I knew what drove you, why you're so willing to hide behind a pretend fiancée when you could easily do what your dad wants—fall in love, live happily ever after in your tower overlooking the empire." Her chuckle was a whisper of sound, drowsy, suggesting sleep might overtake her soon.

"Maybe I like my pretend bride better than the real ones I've met?" He phrased the question as if it were a joke, but the more time he spent with her, the more he wondered. What would it be like to wake with her each morning? To know he could make love to her whenever he desired it, laugh with her, grow old with her? Would the fierce protective nature she extended to the child cover her husband, too? Would she stay vibrant, teasing, or become less fascinating as the years wore on?

Her breathing evened further, her body fully loose and boneless, and he hugged her closer. The peace he searched for out the window and couldn't find seeped in from the scent of Jeanie, the warmth of Jeanie, and his jaw stretched and popped with a yawn.

Resting his eyes, he allowed himself a moment of pretend. She was his, would stay in his arms, and he could just hold her until the sun crept over the skyscrapers and lit the sky in reds and yellows.

For the first time in a very long time, Camden lost himself in the dream until the darkness swept over him…

And he slept.

Chapter Twelve

Kaycee dumped her milk, again, and Jeanie leaped to sop it up before it dribbled onto the floor.

Sophia, one of the maids, brushed her hands aside. "I have this, Miss Jeanie."

"Seriously, you don't have to clean up after her. I keep telling all of you that. It's my job. You weren't hired to keep up after a five year old and — "

Dark eyes serious, Sophia caught her arm. "The fact you don't need us to makes it more of a pleasure. Sit down, eat your breakfast."

With a sigh, Jeanie obeyed. "I meant to ask you…who got the dollhouse? Toys keep appearing in her room." Breaking a piece off the still-warm croissant, she rolled her eyes at how awesome it tasted. When she got back to the real world, she really needed to find a way to include warm croissants in their budget.

"Mr. James sent that piece up, ma'am." Sophia cleared a

plate away, and Jeanie dropped the soft bread onto her plate in annoyance.

"Seriously?"

"Yes, seriously." Camden swept into the room, eliciting a squeal from Kaycee, who leaped up and ran at him full speed.

"Kaycee! You can't keep running at people. Not everyone is going to catch you." Jeanie watched in frustration as Camden did just that, scooping the little girl up and twirling her before settling her back on her feet.

Avoiding her gaze, Camden found a place at the table, waved at the help to dismiss them, and sat down like he owned the place.

Which, of course, he did. Usually, he didn't interrupt their breakfast routine, though, mostly pretending to respect Jeanie's wish for him to stay away from her child.

"Good morning, Jeanie." Finally willing to make eye contact, he pinned her with an expression so intimate and comfortable, she decided it was her turn to avoid looking at him.

"Camden." Fiddling with her fork, it took her a second to remember her annoyance over the toys. "You can't keep buying her stuff. For one, it's not in our contract. For two, you're going to spoil her. If you make every day Christmas—"

"If you make every day Christmas, then every day rocks. Kids are only kids for a minute. It might as well be fun." Accepting a cup of coffee from Sophia who'd reentered the room, he smiled at the woman before dismissing her again.

"But—"

"My vacation has been more fun with the toys," Kaycee inserted. Dunking a slice of toast into an egg yolk, the child was oblivious to the adult tensions circling above her blond curls.

"Vacation?" He seemed interested, his dark brows arched toward his hairline. "You're on vacation, Kaycee?"

Opening and closing her mouth, Jeanie tried to figure out how to tell him about her cover story to the little one.

"Yes, Mommy says this is our vacation. We didn't go anywhere though, but here." Thunks sounded from under the table as she swung her legs, feet knocking into the chair. "My friend, Jessica, she went on vacation and she saw an elephant. I'm hoping Mommy takes me to see an elephant before our vacation is over."

Camden spoke very seriously. "She probably will. Your mama is probably a hundred times cooler than Jessica's mom."

Kaycee giggled, and Jeanie smacked the table. "Camden…"

"Yes, right, we have work to do. Kaycee, do you mind if I borrow Mommy for the day?"

"Sure. Make sure she comes home for my bedtime story." The thunking paused as she carefully reached for her milk glass, nearly toppling it again.

"Will do." He pulled Jeanie's chair out. "Ready to hit the road?"

Sighing, since arguing with him didn't seem to get her anywhere, she stood and followed him out of the room. "I really wish you'd respect my wishes and stay away from her."

"I'll write you up a list of my wishes, and when we can accomplish any of them, I'll start work on yours. In the meantime, we have a problem." He strode through the maze of hallways and led her to the elevator. His long legs ate up ground, making her almost jog.

"We do?"

"Yes, we actually do."

He paused, and now he had her attention. What was such a big deal that the Penthouse Prince would hesitate to tell her?

"What is it?" she said.

Finally he said, "My father announced that we're getting married this weekend. That the engagement party would be Friday. He did so at a very important gala last night, with most of the major press watching, and it's gone viral."

She raced to keep up and slipped into the elevator right before the doors whispered closed. "So, have your lawyers found their loophole? Or what is your plan?"

He met her eyes for a second, then his gaze slid away. "No plan. No loophole…it looks like we have an engagement party to attend."

Last night, she'd felt so close to him. Like maybe they were from different worlds, nothing in common, but maybe they had a connection.

Maybe he was more than his sum parts, and so was she, and together…

But it was all a game to him, and who knew how far he would play it to get what he wanted?

Swallowing, feeling stupid for almost allowing herself to get wrapped up in the illusion, she searched for the right words. "Maybe…"

The elevator dinged, and he buzzed out, apparently using his extra energy from his night's rest to become even more erratic than normal. "Come on. We need to hustle."

She raced to keep up with him, but once at the car, she

stopped to allow him to open her door, then slid inside.

"We're late," he added, climbing in on his side.

"Maybe the solution is easier now."

"Huh?" He put the car in gear, backed up, and then sped out of the parking garage.

"Maybe—"

Her phone buzzed. Annoyed at the interruption, she thumbed it to life and read the texts.

Quit ignoring me. I know where you are. Meet me for coffee, right downstairs from your little love nest, noon. Or I could come up…your choice. Don't be late.

She swallowed hard, then replied. *I'm not sure if I can meet you there. Give me some time. We'll meet, I promise. I'm not sure if I'll be at the building at that time, though. Can you give me another day or two?*

The response came back in seconds, or a lifetime, Jeanie wasn't sure. She focused so hard on the phone, she didn't know.

Fine. But soon, very soon. You know what happens if you let me down.

Exhaling in relief, she pocketed the phone and concentrated on remembering how to breathe, slow and steady.

"Who's texting you?" He leaned over, as if he would peek over her shoulder.

"None of your business." The snapped response wasn't deserved, nor was it fair, but she couldn't let him find out.

Not with so much riding on this working out.

He nodded, not looking her way. "So, you were saying— about the other problem?"

Closing her eyes, she pushed the words out on a rush. "Tasha is here now. You know, your real fiancée? So, basically, you don't need me anymore."

Chapter Thirteen

Telling. His response—or lack of response, in this case—to her bringing up Tasha's reappearance on the scene spoke volumes.

She knew the job would end, that she'd find herself back in the real world and only be able to glean what she could about the rest of his story from the glossy pages of a magazine, but she didn't realize she'd be hurt when it happened.

Not that she blamed him. His fiancée could only be described as stunning—black hair, gold skin—a perfect, gleaming bookend for his dark hair and blue-eyed handsomeness. Tasha belonged in this world, a poster child for the rich and elite, while Jeanie could only fake it.

Appearing at her side with a paper cup of coffee, Lowe studied her. "What did he do? I'll kick his ass for you."

Laughing, she accepted the caffeinated offering and sipped. "What makes you think there's trouble in paradise?

Am I that transparent?"

"I think that's what I like most about you, Jeanie. You would suck at poker, but your face doesn't lie. Spend enough time around these goons and honesty becomes the rarest gem."

"Jaded, much? No, honestly, nothing is wrong. I just foresee the end of my stint as Mrs. Penthouse Princess-to-be and I'm planning how to land on my feet when he shows me to the door." Blinking fast, she swallowed a larger gulp of the sweetened java, hoping he'd think the money ending made her a bit sad.

His hand clasped her shoulder, his eyes soft and full of understanding she should rebuke. "No one is that good of an actress. You feel something for him. Why don't you try something novel—you know, tell him? What could it hurt? Besides, as his best friend, I can tell you a little insider secret…" Leaning closer, he whispered, "He might like it."

Snorting, she glanced up at the man in question, who was holding scissors above a red ribbon for the rededication of a building. Even from here, she could almost feel his gaze on her, a warm touch that sizzled her ability to think rationally. "He doesn't need me. Not now. I'm not sure why he's stalling, but Tasha is back. I mentioned as much in the car, and he didn't answer me. I think we both know what *that* means."

Lowe went quiet and stared at his shoes. "I wonder… do we?"

"What do you mean?" But the ribbon was cut, and the crowd stood in applause. With a quick leap, Camden was off the stage and shaking hands, making his way to her side. Once he joined her, he shot a quick glance at Lowe before hustling her back to the car.

"Today is booked solid. We're basically just going from event to event. That coffee enough, or do you need me to stop for some lunch?" It seemed like just business, him making sure she was comfortable, but when he glanced at her, she saw something genuine in his eyes.

"I'm good," she said. "Why don't you have a driver? I keep meaning to ask—"

"I like my privacy." The statement rang with honesty while being completely strange at once.

"Privacy? You've had me with you for stuff like this ever since you hired me. I'm sure you don't need your fiancée at all of these events...so isn't it messing up your alone time?" She didn't mention going to him in the darkness. Something about those moments, stolen moments out of time if she stuck with his limo summation, was too private to be brought up in the light of day.

"No."

She picked at the top of her coffee cup. He never gave one-word answers. He seemed so willing to fill the air with words, as if to distract everyone around him, the one-word answers just never happened.

Yet to her invading his private time? Just one word. *No.*

He captured her palm in his and stilled her nervous fingers. She glanced over to see his profile, jaw clenched and a single muscle ticking.

She leaned back in her seat and allowed the silence to fill the car and held his hand.

Maybe the reason he'd not yet evicted her from her position was he liked having her around?

Ridiculous, but a warm sensation filled her chest. It'd

been a long time since someone wanted to have her around. She'd just live in that illusion until it popped like a soap bubble, because maybe…she didn't like being alone, either.

. . .

Seeing Lowe and Jeanie, standing close and laughing, sent jagged waves of glass-filled frustration to slice at his chest.

Tasha had nailed it—Jeanie would be better off with someone like Lowe. Someone who understood her, would be willing to risk everything to show her he loved her, someone who wasn't living a life devoted to revenge.

Just because Tasha was right didn't mean Camden was willing to give Jeanie up.

She might be better off with Lowe. She might be better off far away from their world, quietly raising Kaycee until some nice run-of-the-mill man came along and realized what a treasure they both were and scooped them up.

But it didn't matter what was better for Jeanie. She'd signed his contract, she wore his ring, and she lived in his house. She'd made her choices, and now he'd see she lived with them. She was his, for better or worse, and he wanted to keep it that way.

He couldn't just marry her, not even after his father had made that announcement to force his hand. He couldn't rightfully expect Jeanie to agree to such a thing. She'd only agreed so far because he'd assured her this was temporary.

But part of him wanted her to marry him. To make their temporary arrangement last a while longer. They didn't have to stay married forever. But to be with her as man and wife, even if only until his lawyer found the loophole…

Meanwhile, the world waited with baited breath for the bachelor of the year to marry.

What was he going to tell her?

Not my fault—insert innocent shrug—you're just going to have to stay with me forever.

And her throwing Tasha's return at him? How could he answer that without revealing he could give a flippety fuck less about the woman who didn't hold a candle to Jeanie? So...he didn't answer.

Couldn't. He played the situation to keep from revealing to her how much power she currently wielded. Sacrifice that tasty tidbit and let her know she mattered?

Stupid. No intelligent man let a woman know she gained value—that she could rock his world with a frown. Better to keep the deck stacked in his favor...

Her silence and her hand warm in his caused him to cast a glance her way. A small smile played across her lickable lips, and her eyes were closed, as if she found peace in his presence.

He couldn't admit to her how much it meant that she'd curled up in his arms last night. Waking with her still snuggled close, he'd wanted to lift her up, carry her to bed, and watch as her passion awoke with sleepy fire.

Instead, he'd let it go. Let *her* go.

He wondered if she'd come to him tonight. He wondered how long he could resist the temptation of her skin and simply enjoy the ease of her comfort with him.

Not long. Even now his body screamed for him to take her, claim her, feast on her flesh until she forgot everything but the pleasure he knew he could bring her.

But long enough, he hoped, to make sure she couldn't

leave him.

Planning. Leaning back in his seat, he relaxed muscles gone tight with sexual frustration. This situation was all about planning. He just needed to stay one step ahead and it would all go the way he wanted.

Chapter Fourteen

The sun, beating hot on her back, caused the suit jacket over the creamy blouse to itch. Hunger cramped at her stomach, a testament to the hour, and a headache crawled behind her eyes from too much caffeine, too little sleep the night before, and too much sun and fake smiling.

Camden stood in a group of important men, discussing a deal, and she waited. He looked, of course, like the day wasn't taxing him in the least—white dress shirt unbuttoned at his neck crisp as when they'd started, dark denim falling perfectly to his shoes and smile as fresh as when he woke. If the man sweated under his suit jacket, she couldn't tell— then again, perhaps he just controlled his body to the point that not even his sweat glands dared disobey. She'd spent the day waiting, not sure why he suddenly wanted to drag her to every single appearance he needed to make, and longing to go hide in the nursery with Kaycee.

Her calves ached, not used to the higher heels deemed

appropriate for her position by his side. Her lower back throbbed and she would give anything to be wearing a pair of jeans and a tee shirt.

She wasn't made for his world.

Her phone dinged, and she read another text. *Today? Or are you stalling until tomorrow?*

Her real world called, biting her in the ass. She sighed. *Tomorrow. He's got me traveling with him today. I can't get away without it being obvious*, she responded.

His hand closed on her arm, and she stuffed the phone into her pocket quickly, not sure if he'd read over her shoulder or when he'd appeared. "What?" she snapped.

Raising his hands in a peace gesture, Camden backed up a step. "I wanted to tell you we can go. Figured we'd have dinner at home tonight…"

"Whatever." She turned her back on him and stalked to the car, not really caring if he followed. He would go back to Tasha. She would deal with repercussions from this whole stint—she just wasn't sure what cost would be demanded. *What if it was all for nothing?*

Swallowing back the horrifying possibility, she slid into her seat and slammed the door closed.

He joined her after a moment, but he didn't turn the key. "Are you okay?"

"Fine. Dandy. Just fucking wonderful, Prince Charming. Please, just…take me home."

He didn't answer, but finally he started the car. "I think I need to feed you more often. You get snarly when you don't get your meals." His tone suggested he was joking, ribbing her to lighten the mood.

She wasn't in the mood. "I'm not a child, Camden. You

can't just feed me and think it will end an argument."

Silence filled the car.

"We're arguing?" he asked. "I think I missed that. What are we arguing about?"

"Nothing. Just, argh. Shut your stupid rich face up, okay?"

He waited a beat. "My stupid rich face?"

She didn't answer. He pulled up to his building. The doorman moved to grab her door, and she slammed it open, nearly hitting him. Bouncing out, she rushed through the lobby.

Camden caught up at the elevator. "So, we can agree that you're cranky, is that a fair statement?"

"You're still talking."

"Hmm…"

She shot out of the elevator and into the penthouse.

Lowe waited for them, his brows furrowed in unhappiness. "Uh, we have a problem."

Rubbing a hand over her face, she muttered, "Do you need me for this, or is it business stuff and I can have a minute?"

"Sorry, you might want to stick around for this. You're the problem," Lowe answered. With a flick of his wrist, he punched a button on a remote, pulling up the news.

"Today was a busy day for the Penthouse Prince. Starting at a rededication of the MacArthur building, he and his lovely, but unknown until a few weeks ago, fiancée traveled from event to event. Things got really interesting a little while ago at the construction site of the James wing of the hospital. Our crews caught this little exchange between the, up to this point, perfect couple."

The screen shifted from the smiling face of the reporter to the construction site. The camera focused on Camden, shaking hands and smiling, but then panned to her when he moved to join her. She held her phone, attention obviously not on him, when he took her arm.

She yanked it away from him, hiding the phone in what looked like a guilty movement, before scowling up at him. After a moment, she stomped away and left him looking a little lost as he stared after her.

The reporter came back on, but a buzzing filled Jeanie's head.

"You saw it here first, folks. The most wanted bachelor might soon be looking to mend his broken heart. I'm sure the available ladies will be lining up for that job." The reporter's smile was just a little leering, and Lowe shut the television off with an audible *click*.

"So, as you can both see, there's a little hitch—"

"Yes!" Camden punched his fist toward the sky before slamming it down. Then he pointed at her. "You *lost*! I told you I'd win."

"Lost?" Lowe looked confused, and Jeanie swallowed hard.

The headache battled with dizziness. *This isn't happening. Not for real.* "You can't…the bet? Really? But Tasha—"

"Really, Jeanie? You're backing out of the bet once you lost it? You know we're on a timeline because of the press leak by my father. At this point? We're out of time. I need to know if you're in or out, because if you're backing out of our deal, I have to figure out something else, fast. You were kind of my last hope, and besides…you promised."

Her first response would have been to tell him she was

backing out. It was a terrible idea, and the bet had been a ridiculous one to begin with. But something about his face and the way he called her his last hope...

"I didn't say I was backing out. I simply wanted to point out the stakes had changed. Tasha is back and—"

He cut her off with a wave of his hand. "Tasha cheated once, and she'll do it again. I don't care about love, but I'll be damned if I stay with someone who betrayed me. She'll ruin everything. She's nothing but a risk to me and what I'm trying to do. You have to realize that, don't you? We have to act fast. Are you backing out, Jeanie?"

She turned away. "I don't know."

He put his hand on her shoulder. She turned around, expecting to see the slick businessman back in action, but there was something else in his expression. Need. And maybe a hint of desperation.

"I'm sorry I came on so strong about this," he said. "This is your choice. If you want to back out now—if this is too much—I'll find another way. But Jeanie...I need you. I promise, I'll find a way to make this work for you. If you'll just help me out a little longer."

She bit her lip, hard, and closed her eyes. Her first thought had been to tell him to hell with his offer, but then she'd seen his face. The genuine plea for her help. He was giving her a choice.

And if she was honest with herself, nothing had really changed from when she'd first agreed to go along with this insane plan. She had nothing to lose. And if it all worked out? So much to gain.

Finally, she nodded. If he was still in, she wasn't backing out.

The smile on his face couldn't have been more genuine than if they were truly in love. "Then it's settled," he said. "We'll do it Saturday. Lowe, clear my schedule for the weekend. I'm getting married." With that, Camden strode out of the room whistling, and Jeanie tried to remember how to breathe.

"Did I miss something?" Lowe asked.

Jeanie didn't answer. *Married.* The finality of the word gnawed at her, and she rushed to her room to try to figure out what to do next.

Chapter Fifteen

Probably, he shouldn't snoop.

Yet he'd told Lowe to investigate the text he'd seen—albeit basically reading over her shoulder—since he felt he almost needed to know more, and Jeanie certainly hadn't been forthcoming with the information.

The text he'd caught a glimpse of over her shoulder in the car chilled him.

I saw you on the TV. We need to make a new deal or I'm coming for her.

Kaycee? What other her would have Jeanie responding in panic every time she read something on her phone?

Jeanie had said they were sisters, but what if there was more to the story? He knew there was something, but words like "kidnapped" bounced around in his head.

His Jeanie wasn't the kidnapper type. And if she'd kidnapped the kid, the person texting her wouldn't be able to make veiled threats. The person would just turn her in or something, right?

The mystery, which he'd hoped would be cleared up by some tactical snooping, so far remained tangled even more with the added information he'd spied on the phone. The email on his own cell phone proved the investigator still hadn't found out more, a disheartening turn of events. It seemed most information could be found quickly, yet his bride-to-be remained an enigma. He sprawled on the couch, trying to hide both his annoyance and curiosity about her, before shouting, "Are you almost ready? We need to get going."

"Coming!" Her breathless response trailed down the hall and, a moment later, Jeanie came around the corner. "You're the one who said I needed to look even more outrageously rich than normal tonight."

He couldn't find words.

Stunning. A description he'd used hundreds of times to compliment women, but the true definition snapped into place when she added a self-conscious smile, just for him. Like old gold, her hair fell in curls, artfully disarrayed like the elegant up do couldn't contain the wealth of shining softness. The gown, burnished copper, made her skin look creamy and allowed her eyes to really stand out. She spun, slowly, and glanced over her shoulder at him. "So, do I pass inspection?"

Swallowing hard, he realized he should be doing something.

Standing. Yeah, I'll stand up.

He found his feet and tried not to stumble over his words like an awkward teenager. "You look lovely, Jeanie." He heard the raspy, husky need in his voice, even if she didn't seem to.

Her smile turned rueful, and she moved to his side. "Sure."

"What? Seriously, you look beautiful. I'm afraid to touch you and rumple you." Which was a flat out lie. He wasn't afraid to touch her...even though he resisted the impulse to do so. He wanted to dive his fingers into the hair, loosen the pins, and watch it fall over her bared shoulders. Then he'd kiss them and work his way up her neck until he could nibble that ever-tempting, full bottom lip.

"Well, thank you then, but we still need to talk. You can't really *want* to marry me." The doors opened, and she pulled away from his arm to lean on the wall.

"But I do." He paused. "Are you reconsidering?"

"It's crazy. I know what you said, what kind of position your father's put you in, but...it sounds crazy to do this." She huffed out the words, her pretty brow crumpling as she spoke.

"Maybe it is crazy. I won't force you to marry me. But imagine, if you would, that we *do* go through with it. You'll be in the penthouse, at least for part of the year. You're not a stranger, not any more. We both get what we want if we do it, neither of us get what we want if we don't, so why not just do it?" Getting out in the parking garage, he rushed to her side of the car to hold the door open.

"You've known me, what? A few weeks?" She pulled up the skirt, and he glimpsed her calves, muscles taut in the strappy heels.

But I knew I wanted you the moment I saw you. I knew I wanted to marry you before I'd known you a day.

He didn't say it, and he faltered a step as he realized it

was the truth. Maybe there wasn't something so impossible as love between them, but he felt something for her. Something true and genuine. Maybe the most true feeling he'd felt in a long time.

He flashed her a smile. He didn't do romantic declarations. Words were weapons, words could be lies, so he didn't bother with the emotional ones. People too often felt the need to respond in kind, even if they didn't mean it, and he'd grown too old and wise to hang his hopes on forced declarations. Better to give a straightforward explanation.

"In some countries," he said, "arranged marriages are common. It's a very modern idea, this need to fall in love and get married based on an emotional and largely pheromonal response to someone. Besides, I like you, we get along, and you look good in orange."

"Orange?" she sputtered.

He laughed at what she'd said as he closed the car door on her side. Then he went to the driver's side, got in, and started the car.

"Orange. That dress. What color would you call it?" He would call it rusty copper or radiant, but orange seemed like the road to distraction, so he rolled with it.

"It's bronze."

Close to copper. "Okay, bronze then."

She blew out a breath, apparently ceding the conversation. Silence filled the car as he drove to the location his assistant had sent to his phone. Once they pulled into the overhanging circular driveway, Jeanie broke the silence. "So, we're doing damage control?"

"Yes, dancing and adoring each other in public so the press can get some pictures of us happy together again. Then we'll head home. You already read to Kaycee, right?"

She nodded. He pulled up, then tossed the keys to the waiting valet before opening her door to give her a hand out. Her gaze, when she looked at him, was beyond adoring. He bit back a smile and advised, "Stop staring at me like that."

"What? It's my blind adoration face." Her lips quirked, her wide-eyed stare not faltering, and he nudged her with his shoulder.

"Less blind adoration. You're supposed to look at me like you love me, not like you're an obsessed fan girl."

Her laugh tinkled out, warming his skin. Cameras flashed, and he smirked. "Better."

"Why thanks, Prince Charming. So can you dance?" The music thumped, a heavy, fast beat.

"Sure." He pulled her on the dance floor and waited.

"Aren't you supposed to move?" She laughed the words, arms loose at her sides.

"Wait for it..." He lifted his hand and clicked his fingertips. The music abruptly changed to a slow and bluesy vibration, and couples slowed all around them. With a smile, he swooped in, tugging her body flush to his own.

"Oh, you think you're pretty damn slick, don't you?" She smelled as good as she looked, and he gave into the temptation to nuzzle at her jaw.

"I am pretty damn slick." He whispered right into her ear, allowing his lips to brush the curve of her lobe. She shivered, and his smile bloomed.

Twisting her head, she considered him. "Ah, so I get the full weight of your seduction, tonight? Be still, my beating heart." Her words might have been blasé, but her cheeks flushed. Returning to his nibbling, he noticed her pulse raced.

"Enjoy it. For tonight, we show them how much we care…" He touched her nose with his own and enjoyed the little catch of her breath as he ducked to lightly brush her lips.

"Does that mean you're going to carry me out of here? Like the last time we went to a dance?"

He took a moment. "Maybe."

"Lowe earns his paycheck, doesn't he?"

The mention of Lowe irritated him. He didn't want her in his arms thinking of another man. "Shh, just dance."

Holding her close, he closed his eyes and enjoyed the way they moved together as the music swelled around them.

Chapter Sixteen

A girl could get used to this kind of treatment. Which, Jeanie reminded herself, would be why she needed to keep remembering the illusion, the fantasy he'd built to get them both what they needed even if it offered nothing she'd always wanted in a marriage. His arms around her on the dance floor, the heady scent of him while he expertly teased and tempted her with his lips and words…

Ice shivered down her spine. The feeling of being watched on a dance floor crowded with people shouldn't bother her — the goal was to be watched, after all — but her gaze darted around, searching for the source.

And there she is…

Seated at the bar, swirling a drink with an olive on a stick, long legs crossed and a smile on her familiar face, the woman toasted her with the glass before standing.

"Can we leave? Like, now?" Pulling back from the enchanting feel of his body so close to hers, she tried not to sound frantic.

"Sure, we've been here a couple hours." Dropping a kiss to her forehead, he used a hand at her waist to maneuver her out of the crowd.

A panicked glance back showed she didn't follow them. Once on the sidewalk, Jeanie sucked in bracing breaths of the cooler air, goose bumps rising on her arms.

"Are you cold?" Camden signaled to the valet before focusing his cobalt gaze her way.

"No, I'm—"

"Let me warm you up while we wait for the car. Photographer, one o' clock." The last bit was added in an undertone meant for only her ears.

Resisting the urge to look, since she had a bad habit of looking at the photographers and thereby blowing any sense of organic reaction, she slid into his arms. "More kissing? My lips are going to get chapped from tonight."

He smiled, a little half-smile, but his face revealed the tenderness she'd come to revel in. Pretend or not, the expression did wonderful things to the butterflies dancing in her stomach. "Yes, more kissing. Much more kissing."

He slanted his mouth across hers and amped up the passion he'd dabbled with all evening. Her legs went weak with the force of his desire. The wall behind her didn't snap her out of the moment, instead allowed her to brace her arms around his neck and feel him, hard and reacting, against her.

"God, Jeanie," he whispered, and his hands slid from her waist to her ass and shifted her higher so he could better plunder her mouth, rub his tongue against hers, and set fire to her bloodstream.

She fell deeper down the rabbit hole, longing to feel his

hot skin against her own. "More," she whispered.

"Dammit." He pulled back, staring down at her. "Car is here. Come on."

The heat in his gaze froze any words in her throat, and she skipped after him, not breaking eye contact. "Camden?"

"Get in." He opened the door, closed her in, and raced to his side of the car.

"C—"

He held up one hand, silencing her, and focused on the road. Speeding, he made it back to the building in record time and, before she knew it, he had her out of the car and in the elevator.

He didn't speak a word, not the whole time, his body almost vibrating with tension.

Did I make him mad, somehow? Maybe I went too far when I pulled his lip between my teeth, but it felt like the right thing at the time...

Reaching their floor, he stayed silent, and she got out, not sure what to say to fix whatever had gone wrong.

She headed toward her room, not daring to look back at him, embarrassed. *It's not like there's a rulebook to tell me the proper way to pretend to make out with someone...*

He spun her around with a quick snap of his hand at her wrist and brought them into full contact. His hot gaze seared her. Her heart raced in response, but she didn't move.

"Fuck control." He lifted her up, high enough her head was above his, and buried his face in her chest in a tight hug. She could hear his breath, harsh as her own, and the thrill of this man—this powerful and practiced seducer—turned on by her went to her head like an illicit drug.

She twined her arms around his neck, hands buried in

the softness of his hair. "Camden?"

His hands slid up her legs, lifting her skirt on the way, and she moved with him until her thighs braced on his hips. He stopped, breathing hard, when the hot, aching part of her encountered the hard ridge hidden by his slacks.

She closed her eyes. Even through his clothes, it was obvious he reacted to her, and the knowledge caused a rush of wet heat to throb between her legs.

Aching with need only he seemed to waken, she waited. Finally, she opened her eyes. His jaw, clenched tight, and his hungry eyes made her heart flip in her chest.

"Tell me to put you down. Tell me not to touch you. Something. But do it fast. I might change my mind."

She opened her mouth, questions fighting to erupt. "I—"

"Tell me. *Fast.*" One of his hands slid up her back, capturing the nape of her neck.

"Don't put me down." She whispered the words, lost in his gaze.

He clicked his tongue. "Wrong answer. My leash? It was short. And it just ran out."

He found her mouth again and drowned her in his kiss. Since his arm held her weight, her hands were free, and she tugged at the buttons of his shirt. The rasp of her zipper sounded, loud over the sound of their breathing and the throbbing of her heart. His hands grazed the curve of her back, and she sighed.

"Jeanie? I thought I heard you come in—oh!" Lori's voice interrupted the fire engulfing her, and she longed to tell her friend to leave, to go back to bed…anything to extend this moment with him.

But he released her, and the sad-eyed man vanished

behind the smiling mask. "Hey, Lori. Sorry we're a bit late tonight. See you in the morning, Jeanie." He turned on his heel, strode from the hall, and disappeared around the corner.

Quite simply, she'd been dismissed. If he really burned from the inside out like she did, surely he wouldn't just walk away like it was nothing? The seamless shift back to business suggested his control wasn't nearly as frayed as he'd suggested...

Rubbing her face, she turned to Lori, still standing a bit shell-shocked behind her. "That wasn't for a camera." The knowing tone in the older woman's voice caused Jeanie to shake her head.

"Don't build castles in the air, Lori. They'll only fall apart. There's still nothing—"

Lori snorted. "If that was nothing, I'd be fascinated to see what your idea of something is."

Not up to debating it, Jeanie passed her. "I'm going to bed."

"As you wish. I just checked in on Kaycee. Sleeping the sleep of the good, the child is fine."

"Thank you. Good night, Lori."

Never one to let her have the last word, Lori added, "Don't be afraid to take something for yourself, Jeanie. You're a good woman. You've sacrificed years for your sister. No one would blame you if you gained some pleasure now and again. Don't sacrifice something that doesn't need sacrificed. Sometimes, for little moments, we get a chance to have it all. Are you going to let your moment go?"

Sighing, she held onto the door, leaning on it for strength. Her dress gaped, unzipped, and her lips felt swollen. "You're forgetting one thing. He's not mine. We're from different worlds."

"Are you? Are you really? I think you might have more in common than you think."

Shaking her head, she closed the door quietly behind her. She knew better, but it was a pretty thought, wasn't it?

Chapter Seventeen

He tried to contain his excitement, but it was hard. The planning that went into this particular venture compared to taking over a company. Delicacy, negotiations, secret plots…

All for a few hours.

It would be worth it. Her face… It would be worth it.

She looked relaxed, her feet resting on his dashboard—which annoyed him the first time she placed shoes on the hand-stitched tangerine leather interior of his baby, a Bugatti Veyron Sang Noir, as if it were a footrest. Since he'd advised her today could be a jeans day, he couldn't help but smile at the sundress and sandals. "It's comfortable!" she'd grumbled. "This luxury crap…it's easier than it should be to get used to it. Plus, I'd hate for the stylist to have cardiac arrest if someone snapped a picture of me in anything less than matched."

He couldn't tell her pictures wouldn't be an issue, not today. Humming, he couldn't wipe the grin off his face. *Better than Christmas morning, this surprise.*

"Why are you doing the evil genius grinning? Where are we going?" She sipped a coffee and considered him carefully.

"Can't tell you. You'll see in a minute, anyway."

"Hmm, mysterious. Why does it make me nervous when you get all shifty?"

"No clue." He whipped the car in a fast spin, then slid through the gates and zoomed through empty parking lots.

"Is the zoo closed today?" She dropped her feet to the floor and leaned forward. "Hey, isn't that my car?"

"Yup." *Good*. Lori had beat him here, as planned.

"Why is my car at the zoo?"

Ignoring her question, he put the car in park and headed over to her side to open the door. She'd beat him to it, a nasty habit of hers, and already got out to shade her face against the sun with a hand.

"Put on your sunglasses," he advised. When she obeyed, still looking curious, he reached for her hand.

He led her through the entrance, and he nodded to the zoo employee grinning at him. Then she saw what he hoped would bring a smile to her face.

"Lori? *Kaycee?*" Her voice rose on the last, and she screeched to a halt. "I thought I told you I wanted her kept out of—"

"I bought the zoo."

She didn't move. "You can't just *buy* a zoo."

"For the day. I closed it for the day. No photographers, no other people. It's ours for the day." She still didn't move or show any sign of response. He suddenly wished he hadn't advised the sunglasses. "You told Kaycee she was on vacation, and she wanted to see a zoo. So I made it happen."

Still nothing. "You're welcome."

"You can't just…" She waved a hand.

Kaycee chose that moment to come running out of the souvenir shop, followed by a zookeeper. Waving a stuffed snake and wearing a cute little zoo hat, the little girl bounced up and down. "Mommy, I got a snake! Can we go see the elephants now?"

Jeanie's head dropped, chin low, and he reached for her. "Give us a minute." Lori nodded, and he led Jeanie a few feet away. "Jeanie? Are you seriously mad?"

He pulled off her sunglasses to reveal tears shimmering in the green depths of her beautiful eyes.

"You've got to stop being sweet. How am I supposed to keep up this charade if you're being so sweet?" The watery words were followed by a slight hiccup.

"Well, it should make it even easier. Look, maybe I should have told you, but I wanted to surprise — "

In a sudden move, she went up on tiptoes and caught his face. The kiss she bestowed on him devastated his senses like none of the hundreds they'd shared in the past weeks. Too soon, she broke the kiss, dropped back to flat feet, and whispered, "Thank you."

He stayed frozen as she went to her child, scooped her up, and turned to the zookeeper.

She'd kissed him.

He realized, with a little shock, she'd never initiated a contact between them. Not once. The free joy in the simple move left him pressing his fingertips to his mouth as if to hold the kiss in place.

With a sniff, he collected himself. He wasn't the kind of man knocked on his ass by a quick thank you peck.

Except…now he was.

Before she'd dropped the glasses back in place, he read the happiness, free and unfettered, on her lovely face, and his chest warmed. *I care about her.*

The realization caused him to stumble. *I want to marry her, and I actually care about her.*

The sun suddenly seemed too bright as his world shifted and tried to realign itself to the knowledge. He actually wouldn't mind their relationship lasting longer—much longer—and the only thing standing in the way of him getting what he wanted would be convincing her their agreement shouldn't be temporary.

Quick on the heels of the first revelation, another epiphany struck.

But she's not in love with me. She's doing a job, being paid to be with me. I don't want her that way. I want her to love me. If she thinks she loves me, she'll never leave me.

All the money in the world couldn't buy love, not that he believed in the manufactured emotion. It could buy a fiancée. It could even buy a wife. But not love.

So he needed to figure out another way to make her want to stay. Not just be willing to, but *want* to. Maybe, if he worked hard enough at it, with time he could earn her love…then she'd stay.

He suddenly regretted the wager, the lies…since they meant she might actually go through with it and marry him, but only for money. Like the other women who'd tried to snag him. Gold diggers, just in it for his fortune. None of them actually cared about him. None of them had any true loyalty to give.

The idea of marrying Jeanie for anything approaching

the same reasons seemed hollow and painfully empty, and he couldn't ensure she'd stay unless she signed on for the whole deal. She wasn't the kind of woman to go through with it, to agree to a loveless marriage for business alone, and she probably deserved to find the kind of man she wanted—one who could love her, but unfortunately he didn't have that kind of emotion to offer her.

Whether or not she deserved better, he didn't want her to leave. His pulse raced, palms going sweaty, as he allowed himself to really consider her just walking away since he couldn't offer her what she sought, couldn't buy what she'd give someone else for free.

Pushing all of it down, to be contemplated later in the darkness, he shoved a smile into place and followed his ladies into the park. Kaycee would have her vacation, just like her mama promised. What five-year-old wouldn't want a zoo to herself, with the ability to touch the animals and her very own zookeeper to guide her?

And maybe, if the day was good enough, Jeanie would kiss him again.

Maybe.

It should have terrified him when he also realized the idea of another kiss, freely given from her, held more appeal than destroying his father.

Which meant he'd need to work harder on this than his other life plans. Glancing at the sky, he whispered, "Mama, I think you'd understand." No answer came back, but the snapping sound from his chest... He thought that might be the ice he shielded himself with since she'd died cracking just a little. Maybe he wasn't dead inside.

Love.

Funny, the one thing he didn't believe in was what he needed to convince Jeanie she'd found in him. More, he'd need to convince her she loved him enough that she'd never leave…

Chapter Eighteen

Riding high on the success of his zoo surprise, Camden whistled as he headed downstairs on the elevator. Due to his many issues with his father growing up, he'd always assumed he'd be as horrible of a parent as his dad had been. Yet being around Kaycee made the idea of having children—previously abhorrent—more appealing since his relationship with Kaycee pleased and satisfied him in a way he'd never expected. .

The added perk of Jeanie's response to his gift left him soaring. Knowing the two of them stayed in the apartment while he headed down to meet with Lowe in the building coffee shop—preparing for naptime, safe at home—warmed him.

Home.

Funny, it'd always been the penthouse or the city apartment when he'd thought of it before, not home. It took Jeanie and Kaycee to turn the rooms into that impossibility.

Home meant family, another pipe dream he'd long ago decided only fools believed in, like love. It seemed the ladies in his life were determined to try to change his mind about a lot of his established truths.

Glancing at his cell phone, he strode out of the elevator, only stopping when a woman blocked his path. Her gray-streaked hair reminded him of Jeanie—what her golden curls might look like in a few decades or so. A quick scan of her from head to toe revealed more similarities—his bride-to-be might look *just* like this woman in a few decades, depending on her life choices.

Could they be related? But that couldn't be. Jeanie had said she didn't have any relatives to call.

Could it be the mysterious *her* in the text messages?

He thought of the terror etched on her face each time a text came in.

Pieces clicked into place, but he was still missing a few integral parts to create a whole. "Can I help you?" Polite, distant, unconcerned. He guarded his tone even as he rattled through possibilities in his mind.

"Perhaps. Do you have a minute, so we could speak privately?" The woman's voice sounded far huskier than Jeanie's, marking her a smoker if he hadn't already caught a whiff of the smell.

"I'm a very busy man…" He trailed off and started to move away from her, but the woman caught his arm. "I'm sorry, do I know you?" He looked at her hand as if it were no more than an irritating bug that had landed on his suit.

"You don't know me, but you will. Mr. James, it will only take a moment of your precious time. I'm sure you can spare that." Sharper edges, gleaming dangerously, marked drastic differences between her and his fiancée. This woman? She reminded him more of himself—a practiced liar and a cold-hearted bitch.

He twisted his lips to keep his irritation obvious. "Vagueing it up isn't buying you more time. If I were you, I'd talk fast before I have security remove you from the premises."

"Fine. You know my daughters." A smile gave away her glee at her hope he'd pepper her with questions.

"I know a lot of daughters. Women have a thing for me. Maybe you should start a fan club. Great talking to you, but—"

"Jeanie Long." She snapped the name out and shifted from foot to foot. "You're engaged to my daughter. And soon, I'll be your mother-in-law. Do you have a minute for me now?"

Her mother? Keeping his face neutral, he tried again to fit the pieces into place. *Still missing bits...* "I think, if you were her mother, she'd have mentioned you if you carried any value to her. Since she hasn't, if you'll excuse me..."

The hand on his arm tightened. "I said daughters, Mr. James. Kaycee Long is also my daughter."

She waited, and he considered her in silence, mind whirring to process the information. He finally asked, "Kaycee is *your* daughter?"

The smile that slipped across her features said nothing about happiness and everything about triumph. "Yes, and if you want to keep up whatever lies you and my daughter are weaving..."

He nodded. She still didn't offer to explain why her daughter raised her other daughter. The dad? He believed

Jeanie—the man probably died a hero. This snake? "Fine, I can give you five minutes. If you'll follow me?"

Leading her down a hallway, he tripped through possible explanations, but none sufficed.

He opened the door and gestured for her to enter the unoccupied office. She did and stood, back to him, and he waited for her to begin. After all, she'd asked to talk to him, not vice versa.

"My name is Calliope Long, since you're apparently not going to ask. I'm not sure how you got tangled up in this, but you're part of it now, since you put a ring on her finger. I'm also not sure what lies Jeanie told you, but I'm here to reveal the truth."

He crossed his arms. "Which is?"

"Their father entered the military when Jeanie was still a very little girl. He came home between tours, but a medic is always needed and our country is constantly at war, so I'm sure you can guess how hard it was for me to be a single mother to an impetuous child, like Jeanie. I raised her, though, on my own for years. She finally grew up, was headed out on her own to go to college, when I found out I would be having another child. Imagine my surprise—no one expects a baby when they're forty. Shortly after I had Kaycee, Garrett died. They held a beautiful funeral for him, and I tried to get past my heartbreak to be the mother Kaycee needed…" She looked back at him, and the woman's green eyes—so like Jeanie's, yet so very not—blinked back tears.

"Sob story, okay," he said. "Poor widow, you. This doesn't explain anything, and I'm getting bored. Can we fast forward to why your daughter is raising your other daughter?" He glanced at his watch, just to further rile Calliope.

Calliope smacked the table—the mother apparently thrived on drama the daughter wouldn't have bothered with—and went from teary to eyes flashing in a beat. "Jeanie doesn't think I'm a good mother, doesn't understand what I gave up for her. She demanded Kaycee, threatened me. She agreed to make sure I would be safe, and I'm not. My home—I'm about to lose my home. How does it make the Penthouse Prince look? If you leave the mother of his wife-to-be homeless, if you don't do a thing to help her? And her, a veteran's widow… I came to you to ask for help, just enough to save my house. Is that so wrong?"

Ah. The pieces finally clicked. "Let me get this straight… your daughter is raising your child, and you wanted *her* to also take care of *you*? What about the pension—oh, are you cheating the government? Collecting checks intended for Kaycee while Jeanie busts her ass to support herself and her sister?"

"You don't know anything. You don't know our family. If you don't help me, I'll go to the press and—"

He loomed over her and got in her face. "Go. You go to the press, and you tell them that you've been scamming the US military for more than five years. You go tell them your boo-hoo story about how mean that woman—" he paused and pointed up "—has been to you. I dare you. If you even attempt it, I will destroy you faster than you can blink."

"Now just a minute here—"

"Homeless? I have a fleet of lawyers who will be on you like white on rice so fast your fucking head will spin." He straightened his shoulders. "Leave Jeanie alone, leave Kaycee alone, and while you're at it, leave me alone. You're small time, no class, and you don't deserve the children you birthed. They're both a hundred times the women you will ever be. If I see one more text come from you to her, I'm coming after you. Every resource at my disposal? Aimed your way. If you want a fight, you found it. Like I said, go to the press. I. Fucking. Dare. You."

With that, he spun from the room and left her.

Chapter Nineteen

They were getting married.

Not just talking about getting married. They were actually going through with it.

Her palms sweated, her hands shook, and she thought everyone must see through her.

Instead, silver trays laden with small hors d'oeuvres and flutes of champagne circled past her on the arms of wait staff as the wealthy and elite gathered to celebrate her engagement. A glance at Camden showed him in his element, cool smile in place, ready to shake hands and clap men on their shoulders. Not phased in the least when an actor paused near them and grinned his famous, heart-stopping smile, or a famous actress asked about their summer plans.

She wasn't sure she could feel like more of a fake than she did tonight.

Threading their fingers together, he leaned close and whispered, "How you holding up?"

"I keep expecting someone to jump out and tell me I'm being punked, but other than that, fantastic."

His laughter rolled over her, and she tried to reconcile the different parts of him. Man bent on controlling a company? Check. Man who rubbed elbows with the glamorous and the elite? Check. Insomniac who could hold her for the whole night and leave her feeling safe and cherished? Check. Man who bought a zoo because a five-year-old was promised a vacation? Check. Man who could make her come alive and...

Memories of the limo and their meeting in the hallway shimmered to life, electrifying her skin. Man who could leave her breathless and a little dizzy with just the memory of his touch? Check.

Which was the real Camden James? All of them? None of them?

She wasn't sure anymore. The more time she spent with him, the more confused she became, and the more tangled in the web of lies she got.

The night wound on, and her feet hurt. She didn't resist when he offered their good-byes. She didn't even murmur a word of dissent as he stood next to her on the ride in the elevator up from the building's ballroom—*because everyone owned a building with its own coffee shop and ballroom*. She kept herself stiff. Neither touching him nor saying a word, she quickly escaped the daunting presence of him to head to her own rooms.

A white dress hung in the walk-in closet—a closet he'd steadily filled with a wardrobe to fit a princess, or the wife of the most eligible bachelor of the year—and she paused to consider it.

Every little girl dreamed of happily ever after. When she was a kid, she remembered believing in handsome princes and men of honor, like her dad.

But she grew up fast when he'd shipped out, and she was left with her mother. Her mother would sell off furniture, jewelry…whatever she could get her hands on to further her own wardrobe and would no doubt wriggle in jealousy if she could glance at the rainbow of expensive costumes—because that's what they were, costumes to make a regular woman into a princess—hanging in her daughter's closet.

The better the clothes, the better man you can snag.

That'd been Calliope Long's motto. Men were like fish. She'd always advised Jeanie to pick her lure, draw them in, and throw the little ones back. Her mother was of the opinion that men only wanted one thing and the one with the best lures drew in the best men.

The echo of her mother's words chilled Jeanie. When she was young, she didn't see her mother for the cheating, manipulative bitch she was. She'd just seen her beautiful mother, who men flocked to and women wanted to be like.

As a teenager, she'd realized the parade of men, while her father fought overseas, meant Mom cheated on Dad. But what could a kid say? Should a child have that kind of power, to be able to destroy a marriage with a confession?

At least it was just her back then, and she could escape. Her father, bless the wonderful man, devoted himself to his family, his wife, his country. Maybe he had his flaws—God knew, he had a broken picker based on his wife—but Jeanie never saw them. She saw a hero. The video chat when she told him she'd been accepted into school, that she'd earned a scholarship…he'd beamed his pride at her.

Then he'd died.

The void of that loss—the knowledge it was just her and her mother forever more—really hurt. She already didn't trust men. Her mother proved time and again that love wasn't something men cared about, since she indiscriminately had relationships with both married and single men while she wore the gold band of her commitment to Jeanie's dad.

Jeanie kept people at arm's length, even before he died, because she feared being blind to the kind of betrayal people like her mother could commit. The loss of the one man who represented *good* and *safe* separated Jeanie from her family, too.

Until she learned her mother carried Kaycee.

Without her father in the picture, Jeanie could only imagine the future of her sister. Drinking heavier than ever before—because of her supposed grief—Calliope might not even carry to term...

But she had. At the hospital, Jeanie headed to the nursery to hold the tiny baby. So pink. So new. So helpless...

And Jeanie knew what she had to do.

Her mother disagreed, at first. "She's my child, Jeanie. Why would I give her to you?"

Until she pointed out her mother could keep the pension, keep whatever the military provided for military children. It didn't matter, she didn't need it.

She only wanted Kaycee.

Jeanie could almost see the ticking, spinning wheels in her mother's head. Jeanie didn't foresee years of blackmail—always something more—but it didn't matter. Couldn't matter.

Kaycee became her focus, her world.

She did okay, too. They had a home, and it might not have been the best home, but it was theirs. Lori became family, something more than Jeanie expected and yet dear and treasured. When they'd first met, Lori had watched Kaycee while Jeanie worked. Lori'd slowly wiggled her way behind the walls, until Jeanie could count at least her as trusted family.

Now, Jeanie stood on the eve of her own wedding. Was it any less a lie than her mother's wedding? She'd married a man who bought and paid for her. The white dress symbolized the childhood dream—the one about a real family, where people cared about each other and the man could be a hero—shattering in the glaring light of reality.

But for Kaycee? If he married her and accepted Kaycee as part of the package, Kaycee would never want for another thing. He could offer her so much more than Jeanie dreamed of providing.

And…she *liked* him. She damned herself for it, but at some point the lie had become fact. She might even love him.

Did it matter that he didn't love her? She'd never imagined she'd be with a man who didn't. But she'd seen couples who had far less chemistry say they loved each other. Was it possible what Camden was offering could be enough?

Swallowing hard, she removed the gown she'd worn that evening, scrubbed her face hard to wash away the tears her study of the bridal gown caused, and pulled on comfortable pajamas.

Staring at the bed, she couldn't imagine sleeping. Her mother loomed—no new texts, but surely there would be more—obviously aware of the coming wedding. Was she waiting? Biding her time to swoop in and ask for more?

And there was the wedding. She'd walk down the aisle tomorrow, say *I do*, and promise to love and cherish a man who she might actually love…

But for how long? How long until he changed his mind? How long until he went back to his normal life, once the shares from his father were secured?

How long until the world watched her fall from the tower, discarded like a sandwich wrapper, because the Penthouse Prince didn't need her anymore?

Unable to sit still a moment longer, she went in search of him and found him not in his nightly position by the windows—likely too early—but instead sitting behind his desk and on a call. He waved her into a seat before rolling his eyes at the caller and obviously trying to bring it to a close. In the moments he worked to end the conversation, her bravado began to falter.

Yet when he sat the phone down and steepled his fingers, she realized it was then or never. "I want to talk about the wedding."

He didn't answer, silently tapping his fingertips together and waiting patiently for her to continue.

"I've been thinking about everything you've said. About your lawyers looking for loopholes and the time running out…" Her mouth went dry, so she swallowed hard. She couldn't tell him part of her wanted to be married to him. Wanted to see where his kisses led and be around when he dropped the mask and the man underneath showed through. Instead, she went the logical route. "We've both been desperate to find a way out of this, but I have decided you were right. This is a good idea, the getting married."

After a moment, he said, "I thought this was settled. How do I know you're not just hesitating again?"

"You'll get what you want, I'll get what I want. I just wanted you to know that I'm on board, that I agree fully to the plan."

No matter how hard she tried, she couldn't force herself to look at him. He'd been the one who pointed out that it could give them both what they wanted, after all, but what if he'd changed his mind? What if his rational brain realized he could find another way, or maybe wait for the Hail Mary pass that would get him out of making a pretend fiancée into a real life bride?

Worse, what if he simply laughed at her, the whole thing nothing more than a joke for him, and she'd just given him the punch line?

He'd stopped tapping his fingers, and yet didn't answer for a notable amount of time. When he spoke, he broke the silence, and she jerked, startled at the sound of his voice in the otherwise quiet penthouse.

"You're saying you'll walk down that aisle tomorrow and agree to be my wife? To make this a much longer agreement and an actual binding contract rather than something I scraped together in a matter of minutes on the fly?"

Since he didn't sound appalled or on the verge of laughter, she met his gaze. His face was perfectly composed and blank.

She twisted her hands together. "Basically, yes. What's the worst that could happen?"

Her mind rattled off a list of things—she could fall entirely in love with him, he could get bored with her and regret his choice, he could meet someone else, someone more suited to his life and lifestyle…

But he nodded. "I did mention that it would work wonderfully for me, since it would suit me to have a wife without the downfalls of being married. We'd both go into it knowing and understanding where we stood rather than being full of the dewy eyed idiocy most modern marriages are destroyed by over time."

He wasn't disagreeing, and being married to him would ensure Kaycee would be provided for, not to mention being married to him wasn't likely to be a bad job. It certainly would have some perks, since if he made love like he kissed…

Heat flooded up her neck, and she would bet her cheeks were so red as to resemble flags plastered across her cheeks. It was a very good thing he couldn't read her mind. "Exactly," she agreed.

"So tomorrow we do it? We get married."

Again, she found herself unable to meet his gaze, so she focused on his collar as she nodded. The collar moved, and she realized he'd offered his hand. Shaking it awkwardly, she gnawed her lips until she'd ensured she regained the ability to speak without stammering. "Agreed. Tomorrow, we get married."

Once the words were spoken, she slipped her hand out of his and practically ran back to her room. Staring at the gown, still hanging in silent accusation, she bit down on her knuckle before moving back to the window to gaze into the night. "Oh, I hope I'm making the right choice."

The cityscape below, though, offered no answers.

Chapter Twenty

Camden watched the last dregs of night slip away as the red glow of the sky grew and, one by one, lights flicked off on the street below.

Today is my wedding day.

He'd hoped she would come to him in the dark. The light under her door never went out, not that he'd paced past it a dozen times through the night. He wondered what she was doing, how she spent her night before their vows. He'd held his hand up, ready to knock, and stopped himself a dozen times, but he didn't quite have the courage to knock.

Today, he'd marry the woman of his dreams, who came with a child he cared about and who made him smile. They'd walk down the aisle, exchange vows…

And then what?

He'd get the shares, cutting his father out of a controlling position in the company. Revenge for the fact his mother suffered from depression for years and eventually buried herself in a bottle to escape her philandering husband seemed like a hollow victory. It wouldn't bring his mother back. It wouldn't do anything except for prove, once and for all, that he could be a bigger bastard than his father.

Whoopdie doo.

He'd coordinated with Lowe to create a honeymoon trip—only the remainder of the weekend away, so they could get back to Kaycee—and the thought of being alone in a bedroom with her left him hard and throbbing. Would she want him to touch her, his purchased bride, or would she rebuke him?

She wanted him, her body told him as much. If Lori hadn't interrupted, they might have made love days ago... in an organic way, rather than an *it's our honeymoon and we should probably have some sex now* sort of way. Did he want her to submit to him simply because he put a wedding ring on her finger?

He wanted her to want him. He wanted the full breadth of her devotion, her love, her protectiveness to umbrella over him. He wanted her crying out his name, begging him for release he would wait to give her...until she lay boneless and trembling.

He wanted a lot of things, and none of them involved a quickie wedding to satisfy an edict from his father.

Sipping a bottle of water—because he wouldn't shame her by being drunk on their wedding day, but was already too jittery to need coffee—he wished she'd come to him. That they could talk, alone. Maybe he'd find the words to make her understand...

No words came to mind. But he felt sure they would, if she came to him. If she walked in the room right then and moved to the window to twine her soft arms around his waist…

Wishing didn't make her appear.

Today is my wedding day, and I'm getting everything I thought I wanted.

But behind that came a more sobering thought.

And nothing that will make me happy.

• • •

She'd dozed off somewhere near dawn. There was, after all, only so long she could cry. Moving to her window, she gazed out, wondering if he stood somewhere in the house doing the same thing. The wedding gown still hung, a beacon of white symbolizing both so much and so little all in one flowing white confection.

A soft knock at the door made her spin.

Maybe it's Camden. Maybe he's changed his mind, or realized how big a mistake this could be…

"Come in," she said.

"Hey, how are you holding up?" Lori peeked in, her hair unfettered around her cheeks.

Jeanie breathed out a sigh and headed into the bathroom. "I'm getting ready. Should be ready for the pre-wedding breakfast shortly. If you want to head downstairs to the coffee shop, and grab me a gallon or two of espresso, that would be swell. I couldn't sleep."

"Normal to be jittery on your wedding day," Lori advised. "Why, when I married my Danny—"

"See, that's the thing. You were getting married. I'm faking it." She couldn't hide the frustration in her tone, and she braced her hands against the counter. Lori touched her shoulder, and she met the older woman's dark, calm eyes in the glass with her bloodshot, puffy ones.

"Is it fake? Once you say the words and sign the paper, doesn't it become real? Hasn't it—?"

"I'm not up to playing Pollyanna today, Lori. But the coffee? That would rock."

Lori shook her head, sadness warring with her usually unflappable expression. "It will all work out. I'm sure of it. That boy doesn't look at you like he's playing a part."

The door closed behind Lori with a soft *click*, and Jeanie blinked back a fresh wave of tears. Apparently, she still had some crying left in her after all. Of course Camden didn't look like he was acting. What kind of actor revealed he was playing a part?

Stepping into the shower, she just hoped she'd manage to keep up her end of the deal for the day. One more day and he'd have his shares.

Then what?

She couldn't begin to speculate about what he planned to do once they were tied 'til death do they part, nor did she want to.

• • •

The pre-wedding breakfast had been planned by his father as one last chance for everyone to crowd them with congrats. Even knowing her part, Jeanie couldn't resist sipping the mimosas with a bit more enthusiasm than normal.

She wondered if she could drink her way into a stupor, thereby erasing this day from her memory.

A throat cleared behind her, and she turned, trying not to dribble the sweet drink. "Yes?"

Gray-haired, stoic, condemnation in every inch of his rich frame, Camden's father glared at her. "You're seriously going to go through with this?"

Pitched low enough that no one would hear his words but her, and yet she looked around, just to make sure no one overheard him. "Hello, sir. I'm sorry we didn't get a chance to get to know each other better before—"

"Drop the act. I brought your mother."

His words sent ice to wash over her skin, chilling her to the bone. "My—"

One sidestep revealed Calliope stood behind Camden's father, her smile absolutely triumphant.

"Yes, your mother. She told me all about your little scam to steal your sister away. Fitting, I guess, that a liar and manipulator chose my son, but his participation in this ruse has gone on long enough. I'm demanding you back down before you've taken this too far. You're in over your head."

She swallowed and shook her head slowly. Lord only knew what lies her mother had filled his head with. This was just the sort of thing she'd worked so hard for years to avoid. Now? Calliope stood there with a man who had the power to mess with Camden's world, not to mention Kaycee's.

"Did you hear me, girl? I want you to nix this little wedding before it happens. I know my son is a fool, but this is fresh even for him. I think we both know how much damage I can do to your reputation with just a word to the press, not to mention what damage your mother can do. Tell my idiotic son you're backing out." The man adjusted his suit. He looked like he was secure in his position.

He shouldn't look so certain. "Excuse me?" she asked.

"I think I made myself perfectly clear."

"Yeah, you really did, didn't you? Your son is neither an idiot nor a fool. A simple Google search shows how you ran this company into the ground, too busy cheating on your wife—who suffered from depression, you ass—to pay attention to the fact your board was robbing you blind. It wasn't until my fiancé, your *son*, took over that you made it back into the black. Since then, you've done everything you could to undermine Camden. He's not a fool or an idiot, sir, and your disrespect of the man I plan to marry cannot be tolerated. I'm all about respecting my elders and would be happy to show you the respect you deserve as his father…if it wasn't for the fact you aren't acting like a father any more than you acted like a husband. So you can—"

The hand sliding around her waist a moment before his lips grazed her ear left her flushing in embarrassment on top of righteous fury. "Dad? Ah, and Calliope." Camden's voice sounded calmer than she felt, and she relaxed into his embrace, facing off as a unit against their parents.

"Camden." His father had the grace to shift from foot to foot, looking slightly ashamed, perhaps, that he'd cornered her. "I just wanted a word with your bride after I was—"

"Lied to by a woman I already warned. Yeah, got that. Calliope, you and I discussed the repercussions of another attempt to blackmail my bride." *Tsking*, he shook his head. "Luckily, I advised my lawyers and my PR specialists this would happen. I've taken steps against you. By the way, a temporary order of emergency custody has been issued to Jeanie already. You should be getting a copy today, if I understand all the ins and outs. Since the medical records verify, and multiple witnesses are willing to appear and testify, that Jeanie has maintained custody for years while you collected government checks intended for your child, I'm sure you'll want to contact a lawyer." He smiled at Jeanie. "I'd forgotten to mention it, darling. Please consider it an early wedding present."

His words sank into her brain. "You knew?" she whispered.

"She made the mistake of trying to come to me when you'd not fallen into her latest round of lies. Big mistake. Huge." He placed a kiss on her neck before lifting his head to his father. "And you're a batty old fool to fall for her bullshit. I saw through it in a blink. You're losing your touch, old man. Then again, you never could tell the difference between a real woman and a manipulator. Now, if you'll excuse us, it's our wedding day."

He spun her away. She leaned close to him and whispered, "You fixed it?"

"Yup."

"Camden, wait." His father's words caused tension to lock up Camden's body, the tight muscles obvious to her as he continued to hold her close.

"Camden?" she whispered.

"I'm sorry." The words shook, and she turned to see his father's face—to see if his tone matched his expression. With his defenses down, the man looked more like his son than any time she'd seen him over the past weeks. "I keep doubting you, but it's because I want more for you. I don't want you to end up like your mother."

Camden shook, fury cutting stark lines into his handsome face. "Don't you speak of her."

"You were a kid, son. You didn't realize… She had a sickness, and it gobbled up her world in huge bites. I tried to keep you away from it, had to separate myself from it or be drawn into the darkness with her. We didn't understand depression back then, not like they do today with their pill for everything. She drank, she wallowed…the weakness of it—"

"Don't. You. Speak. Of. Her." Camden took a step forward, no longer keeping his voice hushed, and guests began to turn, to consider them.

Jeanie squeezed his arms, causing the cobalt of his gaze to shift her way. "It's not worth it," she whispered. "He's not worth it. Walk away."

"Don't attempt to interrupt a family discussion, girl. This is between my son and—"

The words were the wrong ones for his father to choose, and she recognized it, even though she'd only known Camden for a relatively short period of time. "She *is* my family, father. If you'll be so kind as to remember, today is our wedding. She will be my wife. She is my family. And you? You walked away a long time ago."

With that, Camden pulled her away, leaving the ghosts of their past together, while he led her to the elevator.

. . .

He'd fled to his penthouse, but there was no escaping the ghosts of his past.

Damn it. He should've expected the attack from his father, but even if he'd expected it, he wouldn't have prepared for Jeanie to come to his defense. Her reaction touched him—no one ever tried to fight his battles for him.

They'd parted ways, and Jeanie'd left the penthouse to go where he didn't bother to guess, but likely to prepare for the wedding.

Refusing to admit he was waiting for her to return, he paced at the windows and kept an ear out for the elevator anyway. When it dinged, he didn't turn away from the window. Lowe, probably, stopping to make sure he was okay. He wasn't okay. He wasn't forgiving…

Then her scent reached him. Exotic, delicate, smelling like home to him, he tilted his head back to soak it up. She'd come to him.

On his turf, his lair as she'd jokingly called it. He stilled, hoping she'd pass him by and go to her rooms, since he was in no shape to talk to her. Not when his feelings were this close to the surface and before he'd had time to really stuff them down. Her hand closed on his arm, and he snapped his eyes closed, sucking in a breath. He didn't want to talk to her, to fill the air with more plans and discussions. He simply wanted to taste her.

Part of him, some rational part separate from the more animalistic bit that currently had the wheel of his emotions, pointed out he should tell her to go get ready for the wedding. Warn her, even, that he wasn't wearing his polite face, not right then, and that his control had worn very, very thin from fighting his attraction to her.

The thought of those long days and nights of resisting— of walking away when he only wanted to take everything she so causally offered with her kisses and responses—drowned out the rational voice. He ached for her, and she was here.

He opened his eyes and focused on her.

She was standing so close with that single hand resting on his arm. "I'm sorry about what happened down there," she said. "I just wanted to tell you—"

Whatever she wanted to tell him didn't matter, not now. To stop the flow of her words, he spun and captured her waist, lifting her as he turned her to push her against the wall. All she managed was a tiny squeak of sound before he'd captured her lips with his own.

For a moment—a single, horrible moment while he worried she'd not respond, that she'd reject him or push him away—she didn't move as he teased at the corners of her mouth, begging her silently to respond.

Then she moaned, just a little, and her arms wrapped around his neck. He needed no further invitation, slanting his mouth across hers and releasing the grinding hunger which had plagued him since the whole illusion began.

Her body, so warm and welcoming, curled into his, and he cupped her ass to increase the contact. As the kiss deepened, hunger giving into desperation, he spun her and carried her, one destination in mind.

Upon reaching his bedroom, he kicked the door closed behind him, not willing to release her and let her come to her senses. If he was stealing moments with her, they'd be as many as he could get. Releasing her to slide down his body, he didn't end the kiss, starved for the mysterious flavor of her and unwilling to lose even a second of the taste.

She twisted away from his lips, breathing hard. He stilled and let go of her, and his hands clenched in fists. She'd walk away, he knew. He waited for the blow of her leaving.

Instead, her fingers fought the buttons on his shirt, and he released the breath he hadn't realized he held. He helped her remove his shirt, then reached for hers. They shed garments as they stumbled for the bed, and the little rational voice in his mind warned him to stop while he still could.

If she'd haunted him before, these stolen moments and the actual knowledge of what her body felt like under his would be a hundred times worse. It was one thing to imagine how she'd feel coming apart under him and shouting his name. The torment of imagining would pale in comparison to the hell of knowing, for a fact, what he'd lost.

But it didn't matter, not really, not when she was here, she was his, and she'd chosen to stay.

Finally revealing her flesh in the bright sunshine lit bedroom, he breathed out a little raggedly. Lovely. His bride-to-be was even more beautiful than he'd imagined. Stroking his hand down her flesh, he watched his fingers shake at the weight of the moment.

And then he stopped thinking and sank into his fantasy come to life.

Chapter Twenty-One

They should talk about everything that happened. About where they wanted to go, about the coming wedding and the discussion with their parents. Logic suggested she stop him, stop herself, and insist on those conversations.

Although she knew the wise choice was to slam the brakes on the madness overtaking her system, she wasn't quite in the mood to care about wisdom. She always made the right choices, took the safe bets, did the things she should do. For just once, for a stolen moment in time, she wanted to risk it. She wanted him, and damn the consequences.

She didn't know why he'd spun on her, twisting his hand in her hair, and pinned her to the wall like a starving man who could no longer hold himself back. She didn't care why, thrilled that he'd done it. She wrapped herself around him, determined to see this through and give herself over to her carnal side which demanded more flesh, more kissing, more everything.

Dimly aware he carried her, she didn't release his mouth, afraid if he came up for air, he'd rethink and realize what a horrible choice he'd made. That he'd reject her or slide on the cold mogul mask and deride her for giving in to him.

When he closed the door to his bedroom with a click of the lock, her breath shuddered out. She pulled back, searching his face. If she saw even a hint of the sarcastically cold expression, she'd walk away and not stop.

Instead of the icy chill of his distant mask, she saw his lips twisted in carnal need. His cobalt eyes were glazed with passion, and his fists clenched until his knuckles went white. It was as if he fought himself not to touch her and to allow her the moment she needed to escape him.

She didn't want escape. She wanted more skin, more him, and she didn't want to wait.

She fumbled with his buttons for a moment before his strong hands joined hers and released them. Watching the crisp white fabric drift to the floor, she knew there wasn't any going back. Her shirt followed his, then his hands were on her, igniting a thousand fires wherever his touch lingered. Lost in the sensual haze, she found herself naked in moments, laying on her back with him towering over her. His body was as perfect as she'd imagined, and she wondered if her touch could drive him as mad as his did her.

He ran his hand from her neck to the juncture of her thighs, eyes locked on the path his palm traveled, his fingers almost trembling. The tenderness clear on his face made her heart sing. *He does feel more for me than pretended passion!* But then his lips followed the trail of desire, and her thoughts scattered, lost to a miasma of want, need, take.

She couldn't resist touching him, feeling the bunch and

stretch of his long, lean muscles under his heated flesh. While he dropped open mouthed kisses and nibbles on whatever he encountered, she mimicked his motions, pleased when he panted and seemed to get more lost in the glide of their bodies against one another.

When his teasing lips placed a kiss there, between her legs, where she'd so longed for his touch, she cried out his name. He lifted his head, threw one superior smile her direction, and she fisted her hands in the sheets to keep from coming up off the bed. Then he suckled and nibbled, and stars burst behind her eyelids. Lost in the cloud of desire, she arched her hips into his touch. He climbed up her body, and he continued his decadent teasing with his fingers.

"Please," she begged. "Camden."

"I can't resist you anymore, Jeanie. I tried to give you what you want, but right now? I'm taking what we both need."

She couldn't find words to answer him, didn't know what she'd say if she could have spoken past her body's desperate demands. Luckily, he didn't require a response, and she felt his hardness press against her aching emptiness as his mouth again found hers.

She pushed up into him, starving for more.

He lifted his head to whisper, "Slowly."

But then he was inside her, almost too big, and she bit her lip to keep from complaining. The throbbing pleasure died out, and she fought to stay still and not wriggle away from him. Shocked pleasure shot, lightning fast, over his expression. It vanished to be replaced with a mix of concern and fragile control. He slowly rested his forehead on hers, and their breath sped out in tandem.

"I'm sorry. Are you okay?" Tangled with the concern, glimpses of the triumphant glee on his face told her he knew she'd saved herself for him—for this stolen moment out of time. His fingers brushed her hair back from her forehead. She closed her eyes, breathed through the over full sensation, and finally gave in to the need to try to escape.

But the motion of her hips moving away from him sent a new and delicious wave of pleasure to ripple like a warm wave of tingles from her toes to the roots of her hair. She gasped at the feeling and dug her nails into his back.

"Oh," she whispered.

"Don't move. I'm trying to give you a second to adjust." His warning fell on her uncaring ears as she pulled back a bit further before shoving herself closer to him. If the feeling of him coming out of her body was great, the feeling of him sliding back in was even better. Moving in an almost circular motion, the liquid heat increased, and she bit down on his shoulder to keep from groaning at the wonder of it.

His soft moan told her it felt good for him, too, and she met his eyes. "I don't want to stay still. Do you really want to?" She again shifted her hips, but this time, he seemed unable to resist joining her, increasing the motion with the lift and press of his own hips.

He kissed her, hard and fast, before sliding his fingertips between their bodies to tease at the ball of nerves that ached for his touch. Then he moved faster, plunging in and out of her, and she focused on meeting his motions, eyes closed as the spiraling electricity and erotic tension wound her tighter and tighter. He made love like he'd danced, challenging her to keep up and rewarding her enthusiasm with a blend of passion and tenderness.

The band of need finally broke. She flowed over the peak and shattered into a thousand fragments of light as her body quaked with release. Only somewhat aware of his matching cry and the trembles wracking his body, she let the cloud of bliss roll her under and tried to remember how to breathe without the air shuddering out of her.

He moved away from her, but then took her with him. He soothed her with long strokes of his hands up her back, and she allowed herself to rest in the cocoon of his scent blended with hers. He nuzzled at her neck, and she snuggled into the contact. His voice, when he whispered in her ear, didn't sound like it normally did. "Where's Kaycee?"

"With Lori. I texted her before I came up. She's fine."

His concern for her child warmed her. The languid peace from the orgasm weighted her limbs entangled with his, and she burrowed further into the security of his embrace.

"Stay with me," he whispered.

Hope blossomed in her chest, even if she knew better. Even if she knew it still might all just be a game for him. She nodded, unable to speak with sleep tempting her. She'd marry him, that evening, and maybe she could have security and the fantasy all wrapped up in one tired man.

"Be my wife," he whispered. "Mine."

His words confirmed her thoughts, and she nodded again, hoping she hadn't dreamed it.

Chapter Twenty-Two

The wedding ceremony itself would take place in the ballroom. He would have liked to do a location event, picturing Jeanie on a beach holding his hands. But the situation called for fast, and he owned the ballroom.

He'd worn his fair share of monkey suits, but he still regarded his reflection in the mirror and hoped this one would make her smile the little grin she let loose every so often. The smile, when it flickered across those tempting lips, made him feel ten feet tall and able to conquer the world.

The confrontation with his father should have been anticipated, in foresight. He'd planned on her mother reappearing, attempting to shake their day up and to continue to use her own children to further gain for herself, but his father? Somehow he'd not seen that one coming.

Jeanie defending him? Yeah, another shocker. He'd swept into the conversation, fully intending to rescue her from the sharks, only to find his sweet little bride-to-be using her sharp tongue to flay their parents.

No one ever defended him, probably assuming he didn't need it. He didn't…but the sensation of being defended was more fulfilling than he would have guessed.

And unexpected. Jeanie constantly did the unexpected.

He should regret their moments together, feel some kind of guilt for riding the tide of emotions and having sex before they'd actually said "I do," but he couldn't drum up any negative feelings when the experience only reaffirmed the wisdom in his choice of a bride.

She didn't look happy today, not at breakfast or when they'd parted to get ready. Brides were supposed to glow, to look dewy with love.

Not her. She looked like she was trying to get drunk, hence him giving her space at the breakfast, so she could get cornered in the first place.

Shaking off his dark thoughts, he tugged on a pair of chucks—his one concession to personal style for this day—and headed to the elevator. Jeanie would be getting dressed downstairs, surrounded by a herd of fake bridesmaids and one actual one—Lori—helping her to become fully bridal.

He regretted the continued illusions swirling around a day that really should be them, just them, swearing a commitment to one another. He'd make it up to her, though, once he'd won her blind devotion. He'd give her a real wedding, someday, disguised as a renewal ceremony. But the rings would keep her by his side, so he could win that commitment from her.

It could work.

He hummed in the elevator on the way up, then strode to the suite where her preparations would be taking place. He didn't believe in superstition, and he really wanted a word with her, alone, before they took that walk down the aisle.

He didn't expect the herd of pastel-covered bridesmaids to be mulling about in the hall.

"She kicked us out," Lori explained. "And then that jackwad boss burst in, demanding to talk to her and—"

"And you let him *in*?"

• • •

Jeanie tried to calm her breathing. *Just words*. The coming ceremony would just be words, no more meaningful than any other words, and words couldn't change who she was.

The pep talk didn't help. The intrinsic meaning to the vows, the meaning of the day, left some soft bit of her aching for what would never be, not for her.

Brides took this walk on the arms of their fathers, given away into the waiting safety of their groom's protection. Her dad couldn't be here. Like so many moments of her life, she'd take this walk alone.

"I wish you were here, Daddy. I agreed to this, and I'm going to do it. You always said the world could take everything from you but your word, and I'm keeping my promise, even if I'm not sure this is the right choice. If it's any consolation, I think you'd like him. Mostly. After you kicked his ass."

Chuckling to herself while imagining that meeting, she almost didn't hear the soft *click* of the door followed by the sound of a lock. Thinking Lori ignored her request for alone time, she turned, skirt swishing with the movement. "Lori, I just need—"

"Sleeping your way to the top? I should have realized, back when I was your boss, how easy it would have been to shut you up, but then again, you had your sights set higher, didn't you?" Derek leaned on the door and leered at her.

Aversion warred with trepidation, and the combination skittered across her skin like a hundred angry ants. "Why are you here? You don't—"

"You won't believe what I got today... Fired. I got fired today. So not only did you sleep your way to the top—like a whore—you got me canned. I have a family, Jeanie. They depend on my—"

She stormed toward the door, planning to breeze past him. "Save it, Derek. Your family depended on you not cheating your company. If you weren't a thief, Camden wouldn't have fired you. I'm sure he researched my claims. You don't know him, he—"

He caught her and slammed her backwards, and she stumbled over the skirt. *Damned train.*

"Oh, don't rush off. We haven't talked since the day you left on lunch break and headed upstairs. We have *so* much catching up to do. You worked for me for what? A year? Two? Always on time, always so prim and proper, but you weren't prim and proper for your 'Camden,' were you? First name basis with the owner—name dropping, really?"

His breath reeked of alcohol. Unlike Camden, who seemed an altogether happy drunk in her limited experience, Derek oozed menace. Jeanie considered her options. She could scream or...

Apparently she took too long, because he shoved her. Since she wasn't prepared for the altercation to go physical, he caught her off guard and, tangled in her skirt, she fell backwards.

Sharp pain brought gray dots to dance across her vision, obscuring, at least a little, the menacing grin on his face. She opened her mouth, but he was on her faster than she could manage to make a noise. Pain jangled her thoughts.

One of his hands cupped over her mouth and nose, blocking both sound and air. "Shhh, we're just talking. No need to get noisy."

His body pressed into hers, and she could feel his interest—which shot terror through the pain and annoyance. Waiting, she went still. She tried not to panic at the lack of air, but was only able to hold still for a moment before her body rebelled and she fought to get his hand off in earnest.

"As I was saying, my family depended on me. And you're apparently such a good fuck, you can get one of the richest men in the world to offer you a ring. If you're good enough for the big man, well, I should see what all the fuss is about, right?" Derek tugged at the bodice of the dress, and beads popped off and rolled on the floor. Dizziness joined the gray dots, and her arms got heavy, useless to try to pry his hand off her face—

But then he was off her, and she could breathe again. Sucking in huge lungfuls of air, she tried to sit up, to figure out what was going on, but didn't manage to do more than push a few inches off the floor.

The sound of punches, nothing like movie sound effects, still registered, and she pulled up to her elbows to watch Camden, perfect tuxedo rumpled, kicking her old boss's ass.

"Stop," she croaked, but neither man looked her way. She cleared her throat and managed to find her voice and try again. "Camden."

The other man dropped to the ground, boneless as a bag of meat, as Camden rushed to her side. "You okay?"

"Today sucks."

Laughing, he hugged her, and she allowed herself just a moment to relax in the comfort of his scent and warmth. Her gut said things were about to get worse, but for just a moment, she shoved all of her misgivings aside and pretended he actually cared enough to want her to feel safe.

Chapter Twenty-Three

He wasn't used to things going so horribly off plan. He'd calculated and arranged two wedding gifts to make today special for her. He couldn't tell her the truth—he didn't want her to leave.

It wasn't just that the sex was phenomenal. This was probably the most he'd ever feel for someone.

It seemed the least he could do was give her a wedding day she'd never forget.

But not like this. Not in a way that reminded her how cruel the world could be.

Cold fury made him drive his fists into her former manager, the man who'd reminded him that for all his power, there were still times he could feel helpless.

He'd wanted to show his bride that, with him, she could always feel safe from anyone hurting her ever again. And then this had happened.

"Jeanie, are you okay? Did he hurt you?"

She trembled in his arms, so soft and fragile a body to house so much life, and he wanted to rip the man's head off with his bare hands. "I'm okay. He's drunk. I don't think he realized how far out of line he went."

"You're defending him?"

"No, well, not really. I'm so glad you fired his skeezy ass."

The hint of good spirits in her sent a shiver of happiness through him. *That's my girl.*

He couldn't explain. It was all his fault. The emergency custody order—the fact her mother would no longer be able to take Kaycee away from her on a whim—should have given her security. Instead, he'd used it as a weapon against her mother after Jeanie gave him a far greater gift—her defense of him.

Firing Derek? Another planned gift—*look, I fired your old boss. You felt threatened by him, and now he's unemployed.*

Instead, Fruit Loops had attacked her.

Her shoulders shook harder, and he wrapped her closer, wishing he could protect her. Wishing he could fall to his knees, promise to make sure the rest of her days were spent in happiness.

Then he realized she was laughing.

"What's funny? Because if there's a punch line," he said, "I'm missing it." This only sent her into another hysterical fit of giggles. "Are you in shock?"

"No, it's just—" She smacked his chest, laughing so hard she snorted, just a little.

"Seriously, I can call a doctor. Have one up here in minutes."

Tears rolled down her cheeks, and she just shook her

head. Her pretty dress was ripped a little in the front, beads torn off and rolling on the floor at his feet. Her hair was falling loose of the stylish up-do, curls flopping on her pink cheeks as she bent over in her chuckles.

"I'm pretty sure you hit your head," he said.

"No, I'm okay. I'm okay. It just occurred to me that it's bad luck for you to see the bride before the wedding, even worse if you see her in the dress. I'm pretty sure luck doesn't get a helluva lot worse than this, so..." Another round of choking laughs, but the tears competing with them weren't ones of joy. A fist clenched his heart. *Today is ruined.*

"I'm sorry, Jeanie." He reached for her, but she spun away.

"No, really, can you make him disappear? Like have security escort him away or something? I need to fix my makeup, my hair...send the beauty squad back in. They've got their work cut out for them." Glancing down at Derek, she paused. "You didn't kill him, did you?"

"No."

"Okay, well, all that then. And you? Go do whatever really rich men do before a fake wedding. The stylist is going to have a fit."

The tears hadn't stopped, not even a little. Her words choked across her sobs, even as she tried to pretend calm.

"Jeanie—"

She waved him away again, summoned a smile he didn't believe, not even a little, and shut the bathroom door in his face.

He let his forehead rest on the wood. Every woman deserved the wedding of her dreams. His gifts? They didn't fix the fact he'd ruined hers for her before it even started.

Regret and guilt, new emotions for him, curled in a sickly knot in his stomach.

"I'll make this up to you." He promised in a whisper to the door, a vow to go with the others he'd add before the day was over.

He smacked the door, then unlocked his phone and dialed security. He only paused outside the suite to advise the bridesmaid squadron that Jeanie would need help fixing her look.

Striding down the hall, he tried to think of how he'd make it up to her. Although he might not be sure how...he'd keep his promise.

He owed her more than that.

Chapter Twenty-Four

The fake bridesmaids, one by one, took their tour down the aisle, and Jeanie hovered behind the door, trying not to panic. For one, she'd seen the groom before the wedding. For two, she'd been verbally and physically attacked today.

This isn't what a wedding should be like.

Lori held her arm, face concerned. "Are you okay?"

"Why does everyone keep asking me that?" She shook free of her friend's comforting touch and stood straighter. "Of course I'm fine."

Lori snorted. "It's almost my turn to head down the aisle. I'm going to have to leave you. Are you ready for this?"

She could hear the unspoken additions to that question. *Was she ready to walk down the aisle?* Yes, white dress and hair done—good to go. *Was she ready to face the crowd of people staring, waiting to see the Penthouse Prince take a bride?* Sure, whatever. They were all strangers.

Was she ready to swear to love and cherish Camden, in

sickness and in health, as long as they both shall live? Sure. What was one more lie, at this point?

He didn't love her. But he'd shown her he was loyal and would keep her safe. Was it selfish for her to want more?

"Yeah," she answered. She hadn't expected her voice to waver.

Lori sighed, turned, and—bouquet in hand—began her march down the aisle.

Kaycee wasn't there. Her mother and father weren't there. Lori was the closest thing to someone there for her, and she wasn't even really there for Jeanie, not that day. She had been hired by Camden, same as Jeanie.

The wedding march started, and she clutched her own flowers tightly before beginning her walk. Keeping her gaze down, so as not to take in the hundreds of eyes watching to see if she faltered, she put one foot in front of another.

The music boomed, too loud. She allowed herself to daydream, imagined her perfect wedding day. The one the little girl in her had planned so long ago, with her father by her side and friends and family filling the pews. Her dress would be simple, not beaded and heavy like the one they'd done their best to repair before she headed to the ballroom.

Maybe a beach instead of a church, with the sun setting and the waves crashing as her bridal march. Her groom?

Well, Camden's face superimposed the image of her perfect groom, and she figured, since she was fantasizing anyway, his face would have that sleepy, tired sweetness that so tripped her trigger, even if it was just another mask.

She came to the end of the aisle and looked up, but she couldn't bear to meet his gaze and see the mogul mask. Better to stay in the imaginary wedding, where he'd smile at her before taking her hand in his.

Her father—he'd look so tall and brave, wearing his dress blues. The minister would ask, "Who gives this woman to be married to this man?" And her father's voice would break, just a little, when he answered, "I do."

She kept her eyes on Camden's chest and heard him speak softly instead of the ghost of her father, repeating the words of the man doing the ceremony. "I, Camden James, take you, Jeanie Long, to be my lawfully wedded wife, to have and to hold, to love and to cherish, from this day forward, for better, for worse, for richer, for poorer, in sickness and in health until death us do part."

His voice didn't quaver, sounding so sure as he swore promises to her he had no intention of keeping. The complete surety in his tone finally tricked her into tracking her gaze up, to consider his face.

Just like in her imagination, his expression held tenderness. Then again, of course it would. He *was* acting. The man was a master liar.

But at least with what mattered, he'd been completely honest with her. He hadn't made any false declarations of love. He'd told her upfront what he could offer and why he wanted her.

The ceremony continued, and then it was her turn. She couldn't look away, not once he'd captured her with his cobalt gaze, and she tried to inflect the same confidence he'd displayed into her own tone.

Her voice only quavered a little while she vowed, "I, Jeanie Long, take you, Camden James, to be my lawfully wedded husband, to have and to hold, to love and to cherish, from this day forward, for better, for worse, for richer, for poorer, in sickness and in health until death us do part."

More words, but she didn't hear them, not past the buzzing in her ears.

His smile took her breath away, for just a second so open and trusting that she sailed away on that twist of his sarcastic lips.

And then they must have said he could kiss her, because he swept her into his familiar embrace and took her lips.

It was done. She was his wife.

Applause broke out, and she stayed in his arms and didn't look around. There was no one here for her, besides him, so they didn't matter. Perhaps the faked wedding was the best she could hope for, all things considered. Maybe she'd always wanted the fairytale, believed in it deep down, past logic and cynicism, but she'd seen enough of the world to know not everyone got what they wanted, so maybe this was it for her. In this moment—maybe it would all work out. Maybe the illusion could be real enough to become reality.

Chairs were cleared and music piped over the speakers. She recognized *Marry Me*, locked in the arms of her prince, and allowed him to glide them across the dance floor.

She'd just keep playing pretend for now.

But then she thought of Kaycee. Her child in every way that mattered. What would this mean for her? What would she think if she knew Jeanie had married for anything less than love?

Kaycee deserved more than money and a pretend family. How could she hope for Kaycee to expect more from a man or herself if the only model she grew up around was their pretended wedlock?

Jeanie hoped she hadn't just made the biggest mistake

of her life.

• • •

"We're leaving?"

He paused, surprised at the sound of shock in her voice. He'd waited until they got back upstairs, the darkness of the apartment seeming exceptionally quiet compared to the noise downstairs, to tell her.

He'd expected surprise—sweeping her off on any kind of honeymoon should have elicited some startled smiles or something—but the slightly horrified look on her face wasn't what he'd imagined when he'd played this out in his head. "Yes, we're headed off on our honeymoon."

She screeched to a halt and tugged her hand free. "I am not, like, going off with you."

"We just got married. You're my wife. The tradition is—" She smacked his hand away when he reached for her. "Jeanie—"

"Don't start talking about traditions now. The proper way to do a wedding is the man proposes, baring his heart, on one knee. You never proposed, you contracted me."

"But—"

"Nothing about this wedding has been traditional. I sure hope you don't think I'm just going to roll over on my back like a sea turtle washed onto the beach backwards and let you have your, your—" She flailed for words before stabbing him in the chest with her finger. "Your way with me!"

"Did you really just say that? Because it's sort of archaic."

"You know what I mean!"

"I'm not demanding sex, just so we clear that misconception up, although I think we both realized earlier we could enjoy a physical relationship as well as a business one." He wasn't opposed to sex, and being this close to her, yeah, he desired her…a lot. Like more than any other woman he'd ever met. But he wasn't taking her on a honeymoon to force her into it.

If she rolled over and demanded it, sea turtle or not, he'd oblige, but…

"Did you really think a honeymoon was a good idea?" She looked annoyed, not thrilled by the prospect as he'd intended.

He tucked his hands into his pockets and rocked on his heels. He'd thought he made his position evident, that he'd told her he didn't plan to end their marriage. "We kind of have to go anyway, you know. It will make the wedding look more believable if we — "

"Oh." She gnawed her lip and stared at the floor. "You should have mentioned that."

He sighed. It wasn't just for the illusion, but he couldn't exactly tell her that. He'd wanted to be alone with her, to have time with her. Time to explore their feelings for one another without having to pretend for an audience.

"Besides, I hadn't actually planned for us to get divorced. I told you, it's the flawless marriage. One without the pitfalls and traps that usually breaks people up. As a business arrangement — "

She'd just headed away from him, probably to go pack, when he spoke, but she again slammed to a halt. Whatever he'd planned to say died in his throat as she turned to face him. "Forever? You planned on us staying married?

Indefinitely?"

"Well, yes. I'm not planning to divorce you, if that's what you're asking. You're my wife. If you wanted out, I guess…"

"You guess what?"

He couldn't force himself to say he'd have Lowe look into it, not when he didn't really want her to leave. "Look, I've explained that I don't believe in love, but I care about you and Kaycee. I want to see you both happy and safe. You probably don't get this, but I don't want my marriage to be like my parents' and just about everyone else's I know—betrothed one day, and then, because someone didn't meet some unrealistic expectations, everything falls apart."

Part of him wished he could be the kind of man Jeanie wanted, silly enough to believe in pipe dreams like love, so that he could give her the promises of devotion she wanted. If he could, it would be a hundred times easier to convince her she loved him, ensuring she'd stick around.

"I don't want everything to fall apart, either," she said."

He searched her face, eager to see if that meant he had her loyalty. "I would like us to share as happy of a marriage as we can. If I have my way, we'll stand by each other forever."

Her green eyes blazed at him, a sheen of tears adding depth to their already fathomless beauty. Like looking at the fields of Ireland right after the rain, the brilliance of the color humbled him.

"Forever?"

"Well, yes."

She blinked, and tears slipped out. Something flickered in her eyes—for one moment it seemed like hope, the next hesitation—and then she said, "I'll pack."

She didn't say anything more, just left him. He leaned

back against the wall, suddenly tired. He'd said he wanted this forever, and she'd seemed pleased, but he'd seen a glimpse of something else in her expression.

Was this all an act for her? Would she leave as soon as she got what she wanted? Was she just waiting for him to find the loophole?

He knew women only cared about security and money if they weren't telling the pretty lies people were programmed to tell. Lucky for him, he had money and security to offer her. Surely it, and he, would be enough. Enough that she wasn't lying about her loyalty to him. But what if he wasn't?

What if she wanted the fairy tale of love enough to leave him for someone who would tell her the words she wanted to hear?

He'd basically tricked her into marriage. The possibility of a future, of forever, without her stretched out in front of him.

The hopelessness of the idea chilled him. He'd lived in an unhappy home for a long time. He'd been alone practically as long as he could remember. So why was the idea of her leaving and him being exactly as he'd started suddenly so damn scary?

Chapter Twenty-Five

The silence in the car seemed to carry a physical weight. The night, warm and a little humid, didn't help. Rolling down her window didn't offer reprieve, instead left the air to smack into her like a wet fist. She wasn't sure where they were headed, nor did she question him. Instead, she leaned back, eyes half-closed, and hoped she looked relaxed.

Actually, it felt like someone was twisting a rubber band farther and farther out of shape inside her, leaving her nerves ready to snap. "So, do we have to appear on the beach and look like lovers? Or what's your plan?"

"The plan is that we leave. We avoid the press. A couple in love on a vacation isn't looking for photo ops. Just the opposite, really." His gaze didn't leave the road, and he lapsed back into silence. Minutes ticked by, and she counted the seconds of them.

Tapping her finger on the window frame, she asked, "Are we there yet?"

He snorted.

The rubber band distorted further.

After an infinite amount of time—she lost count on the seconds when they stretched into minutes, and then the minutes stretched further—he pulled onto a gravel driveway that led up to a sweeping set of white steps. He didn't bother to come around to her door, instead grabbed their bags and passed all of them but one to a waiting member of staff.

Not even glancing back to see if she followed him, he strode into the hotel and out the back door, headed for a private bungalow set in the sand like a dream getaway. The path, lit by small tiki lanterns, led right up to the door he breezed through. The sound of waves crashing and the crunch of sand under her feet should have relaxed her, but she felt even less at ease. Like a silent scream of panic in her ears, she imagined years of living with him in strained silence…

She followed him inside. So this was it. Her honeymoon. Maybe this would show her if she'd made the right decision. If this could truly be enough.

The awkwardness and distance from the car ride apparently chased them to the room. Tired of the weight of it—of the constant tension of the past weeks altogether—she headed to the bar. An extensive quantity of options faced her, but she chose a nice looking bottle of Moscato.

It looked expensive. Was it okay for her to drink some? *Who in the hell cares?*

She'd seen the way her husband flaunted his money. This was the lifestyle she'd bought into. May as well see if it fit.

She found a corkscrew, located like everything in his life—conveniently—and she struggled for a moment before managing to free the nearly clear liquid. Ignoring the wine glasses, she found a large water glass and filled it.

She brought the bottle with her, chose a chair near him, and began to drink.

Heavily.

The wine was cool, refreshing, and went down quite smoothly. It had been months…no, *years* since she'd been in a position to drink to delight. And the more she drank, the less loud her fears buzzed in her head.

It didn't feel like much time had passed before she refilled her glass, glad for the warm haze falling over her.

• • •

When he'd imagined his wedding day, he'd never imagined a day like this one. Then again, he'd also never expected to care about his bride.

Fucking expectations. None of them mattered when it came to Jeanie.

She'd advised him this wasn't a honeymoon. So it wasn't.

Then why isn't she going to bed? He knew there was only one in this suite, one monstrous bed he'd planned on laying her out on to watch her writhe for his touch. His one specific request to Lowe had been the bed, a hedonistic place for them to explore the passion between them, and for him to tempt her into confessing she felt more than a contract between them.

Instead of sleep, she apparently planned to get hammered. Quietly.

She never offered him a glass, nor did she seem to require any sort of encouragement to continue sipping away.

While he appreciated a drunk woman as much as the next guy—warm, willing, no inhibitions—he could think of more interesting ways for his bride to spend their wedding night, not to mention safer ones considering his intention to keep his hands off her.

Refusing to look at her, he allowed time to pass. Perhaps, if he didn't speak—didn't move, really—she'd tire of his company and take her bottle to bed with her this first night of their wedded bliss. Or fall asleep.

Whichever.

Lord knew, those were the only ways he could resist her.

"You're still not talking to me."

Breaking a promise to himself, he slanted a glance at his bride, who'd slurred just a bit when she spoke. She'd changed into traveling clothes before they'd left the penthouse, apparently thinking a short flirty skirt and blouse were appropriate dress for honeymooning.

Since then, she'd undone buttons on the blouse, leaving the sides gaping to give teasing glimpses of too much flesh. Her lounging in the chair made her skirt ride up to reveal too much tempting thigh. He deemed the glimpses of her flesh inappropriate to his plan not to touch her. "I'm not *not* talking to you. I'm simply not talking. It's been a long day. I'm relaxing."

She snickered. "You look very relaxed."

Okay, perhaps he didn't look relaxed. *Which is entirely your fault, wife.* "I'm quite comfortable. Aren't you?"

He made the mistake of considering her again. She stood, slowly. "No. It's hot here."

With that, she shed the blouse.

His gaze tracked up, unwilling to listen to his mind which

screamed, *Don't look!* But he did—from her bare stomach to her lovely breasts, just contained in a scrap of red—*who in the fuck thought putting her in red was a good idea? The stylist is fired, first thing tomorrow.* She looked...

Delicious.

His wife displayed a sweet combination of innocence and seduction, topped off with a lazy grin and hungry gaze. Her green eyes glittered in the semidarkness of the room, darker, mysterious, and full of womanly secrets he longed to explore.

He swallowed hard. He tried not to trip over his tongue and searched for a snarky response. "Feel better?" Well, it wasn't snarky, but he didn't beg her to come sit in his lap like a letch, so he'd consider it a win.

"A little." She wiggled out of the skirt before dropping back in the chair to stretch her legs out to rest next to his on the coffee table facing the bay windows. "Ah, now that's better." She swigged her glass of wine. "But I'm running out of wine. And I feel a little...loopsie? So I'm not sure I'll be able to open another bottle. Would you be a dear and figure out how to open another for me?"

She didn't need more wine. She was already well on her way to shitfaced. "I'll get right on that." *Stare out the window, Camden. Don't look her way. The booze will make her sleepy, and she'll go to bed.*

His eyes were traitors and sought her flesh. It lay temptingly close and yet too far away.

His dick? Granite. He gritted his teeth. If someone asked him, right then, which he wanted more—a taste of her or his next breath—he would make a really unwise decision.

"You said we'd be married for a while."

Stable ground offered itself up, and he scrabbled for it. "Yes, unless you find that an unsuitable arrangement. I thought that was what we'd both agreed to."

Safe topic. Focusing on the problems would distract him from her drunken...whatever the hell she was doing.

She stood, and the rustle of her movement tempted him to look again, but he resisted. There was, after all, only so much he could take of this delicious torture.

Bad move. She straddled his lap, and he forced his hands not to lift and capture her breasts, now within range. Her movement, a little awkward and somewhat loose-boned, no doubt from the alcohol coursing through her bloodstream, still placed her in his arms, her hands braced on his shoulders for balance.

But he kept his hands to himself. Even as his heart raced and sweat broke out on his upper lip from his internal battle. *Look, but don't touch* became his mantra and looped through his short-circuited brain.

"See, so long as we're married on paper," she said, "I should at least reap the benefits of being married to an international playboy. You've proved you know what you're doing in that arena, anyway. You care about me, you turn me on...I should have more sex, don't you think?"

He swallowed again. Nothing that came to mind was an appropriate response. *Yes, please?*

No, can't say that...dammit.

Theirs might not be a traditional marriage, but their first time together as man and wife should be special, and he didn't want to ruin it. She was drunk, didn't mean what she said, and no matter how much he wanted to...

He finally settled on, "That's the wine talking. You

should sleep."

You should let me suck those puckered nipples. You should bow backwards when I thrust my fingers in those tiny panties and make you howl my name to the sky.

Fisting his hands on the arms of the chair, he prayed for the strength to remember the wine she'd drunk and that she deserved more than he could offer her.

"I'm not a virgin anymore." Her whispered confession near his ear shot a jolt of pure lust through his already over stimulated system, even if he'd known that fact. "That ship already sailed, right? I *was* waiting for the right time."

He could give her a "right" time.

Followed by a left time. Then a bent over this chair and bucking time...

"For however long we continue this..." She waved a hand, obviously searching for a word, "thing we're doing, I'm obviously not free to look for another relationship. Maybe I planned on being with someone who loved me? Who knows if I'll ever find something like that? So, since I'll never have a right time, because I'm married to you now, I figure we should have lots of sex. Maybe then I'll be able to think rationally again." Her lips slid up his neck, and his body responded to the feel of her warm flesh and the scent of her, rich and exotic.

But his mind dropped out of the game like she'd dumped ice water right on his throbbing cock. He caught her shoulders and pushed her to her feet, freeing his legs. He then scooped her into his arms and strode into the bedroom.

"I knew you'd understand. Thanks, Penthouse Prince." Her fingers fumbled at the buttons of his shirt.

"Don't call me that." He gritted out the words before

depositing her into the center of the bed. He paused at the door to glance back at her, spread like his every fantasy on the bed and wearing a sexy smile. He shook his head and moved back toward the bed. "And I'm not taking what you're offering under those terms. If I wasn't the right choice before I became the only choice, I'm not the right choice tonight. Goodnight, Jeanie." Bending, he kissed her forehead. "We both deserve better than this."

With more regret than he expected, he closed the door on her sweet temptation and imagined all the cries he could be wrenching free of his new wife. When she'd sobered up, he'd tell her he wanted it to be good for her, as special as it could be, anyway. That he'd wanted her to remember it rather than forgetting most of it to a drunken haze.

If she chose to give herself to him again, now that they were married, he wanted it to be right for her. She deserved that, and if he couldn't offer her love, he'd at least give her that much.

He headed out to walk the beach and get control of his rocketing sex drive. Eventually, he fell to his knees, gazing up at the sky. "A little help here? I married the woman I need. This should be the happiest day of my life, since I'm getting everything I wanted. So why am I so damned miserable?"

The stars glittered and waves crashed on the beach. The world spun, and a million or billion people kept living their lives while he waited in silence.

But no answer came from the sky.

Chapter Twenty-Six

She woke a few hours later and battled waves of remembered rejection. Once she'd gotten past her temper, she decided perhaps he hadn't rejected her so much as he'd refused her drunken proposition. She decided to find out and braved the hallway to look for him.

As in the penthouse, she found him gazing out the windows at the night, hands folded behind his back. She cleared her throat and swallowed hard when he swiveled in her direction. "Look, about earlier. I wanted to say I'm sorry," she said.

He quirked a finger at her, then spoke in a soft, irresistible voice. "If you've sobered up, then come here."

Wondering if she could set the tone for their exchange, she quirked a brow at him. "Do you really think you can just twitch a finger and have me come, rich boy?"

He allowed his smile to crawl slowly over his lips as he quirked a brow at her. "Depends on your definition of the word, wife."

She smiled, pleased he seemed willing to play along. "Oh, you think you're clever, Mr. James."

"I know I'm clever. Seriously, come here, please?"

Something about the sight of him, all raw and tired, and the gruff edge to his voice when he said *please*, twisted inside her heart. Dammit, could she have fallen in love with him? Even as she told herself she couldn't, even as she knew it was only a job? She couldn't love him.

The possibility shoved her into restless movement to join him at the windows. They hung open, the sea beyond waving merrily against the beach as it glittered in moonlight as if someone hung the water with stars. Gossamer curtains wafting inward brought the warm smell of a salt-scented breeze.

She simply *couldn't* love him. But she also couldn't resist him.

She turned to him, stopped only inches away. When he made no move to touch her, she toyed with his hair. "Was it that I drank or what I said that made you leave me alone in our bed on our honeymoon? Or something else…like, well, you didn't want to." Unable to look him in the eye, to risk seeing something she didn't want to see on his face, she began fiddling with the buttons on his shirt.

He shrugged, considering her question while his hands began to explore her back and sides. Just his touch sent shivers of need dancing across her skin, and her pulse began to thud the way it did only when he held her close. "I thought we both deserved better than a roll in the sack that you wouldn't even remember tomorrow. I'd like it if you remembered me, us, this…"

His voice trailed off, but his lips on her neck made up for the lack of words. Tugging him closer, she whispered, "I don't think I could forget you if I tried, Camden."

Because, at some point, the act had become reality for her. From his laugh—and all the different forms it could come in, ranging from cold sarcasm to warm and unfettered joy—to the way he smiled, to the funny way he shoved out all his words in a rush like someone might stop him from speaking. All of it. His random act of awesome in buying a zoo…his arms as he held her…and the epic wonder of his mouth on hers, lighting up her nerves like they were fireworks and he the match. *Love.*

Emboldened by the realization, she claimed his mouth with her own, determined to show him all he meant since she couldn't possibly come up with words to encompass the breadth of her feelings.

• • •

As if she'd snapped the tether he used to hold back from touching her, he streaked his hands across her flesh like a starved man at a banquet. When her greedy touch seemed as desperate as his own, he smiled.

She grazed her nails down his chest and watched his face closely to see him react. He didn't hide his growing desire from her. When her fingertips paused at his belt line, he shifted them to the couch to allow her the time to explore and become comfortable with him.

But his own passion didn't afford him the time to stay still as she explored, not by a long shot. He tugged the bra down so he could give the hardened nipples more attention.

She sighed, and her hips shifted against him. When her gaze again locked on his, he watched her bite her lip. The challenge in her eyes was clear.

Her busy fingers removed his shirt and undid his pants. He trailed off his own touching, distracted by her mouth as it teased lower until she knelt on the floor in front of him. Her breasts free of the bra, but held up because he'd not removed it, rose and fell with her panting breaths and her lips turned up in an impish smile as she grazed her nails lightly over his throbbing bulge. "You're becoming quite a tease, Mrs. James," he told her.

She laughed. "It sounds so weird to be called that."

The temptation of her wrapping her red lips around his cock diminished. He imagined being deep inside her when she laughed, imagined all her muscles clamped around him. He tugged her up, eliminated the barrier of her underwear, and pulled her back to straddle his lap.

Her amusement disappeared when slid his fingers into motion in her hot, wet cleft. He wasn't sure he'd ever tire of how responsive to his touch his wife proved to be. As her head lolled back and she rocked with his touch, he whispered, "Get used to it."

He spread his legs farther to grant her access when her fingers sought his cock. She shoved his pants down around his knees, didn't bother to even pull them all the way off before she cupped his over-sensitive shaft in her hand and rubbed it against her waiting heat.

Impatient, he brushed her hands aside before lifting her and thrusting deep inside.

For a moment, time stopped. Suspended in the completion of being buried deep inside her, he nuzzled her ear and dropped kisses wherever he could reach as her deep breaths tickled the hair at his neck.

Then she moved. Her hands cupped his cheeks, demanded his mouth, and their tongues tangled. Her hips rose, found a slow rhythm, and he tried to distract himself from the pleasure. She managed to get him so close to losing all control with so little effort, he needed to concentrate to ensure she gained her pleasure before he surrendered to his own.

She braced her hands on his chest, then increased the speed and power of her movements. He caught her hips so he could rise up to meet her. Her head lolled back, and the golden cascade of her hair brushed his hands as he increased the speed. A shift of his hand allowed him to jiggle the sensitive bundle of nerves between her legs, and he swallowed down the triumph he felt as her lips opened to release soft moans and her rhythm became unsteady. She was close.

He leaned forward to suckle her nipple. Her cries became words. "Camden. Yes, please, yes. God, I love you."

They both froze.

Her head came up slowly. He backed away from her flushed breasts and met her gaze as she blinked and tried to focus. He didn't want her to focus. *She'd said it.*

"Say it again, Jeanie."

She shook her head, hair lit by the moonlight to resemble treasure spilled from a long buried cask. Her heavy bottom lip stayed clamped between her small white teeth as he changed the angle, swiveling deep inside her as he fluttered his thumb against her clit.

"Say it." He repeated the demand, and her shoulders

arched toward him. Her hands found purchase on his arms, and her nails bit into his skin. He closed his eyes to keep from coming and losing the moment.

Still, she didn't answer even though her breath came hard and her body bowed into his, begging for release.

"Please." He bit out the word, knowing he couldn't hold out much longer.

"Love you," she chanted. "Love you, love you." With each thrust, she repeated it until he claimed her lips and swallowed her shout as she shattered around him. The muscle spasms of her orgasm milked him, and he felt his own climax rock from the balls of his feet to the roots of his hair. Pulling her close, as close as he could get her, he surged one last time in both triumph and release.

He snuggled her close, didn't let her go, stroked her back and peppered kisses between deep breaths. "Thank you."

She'd stay with him. She'd admitted she loved him. The satisfaction of the sex wasn't anything compared to the relief of knowing she would not leave him. If she loved him, she'd never leave him. It simply wasn't how she was wired.

For a long time, they lay together in the darkness, and he reveled in the knowledge he'd won her heart.

. . .

Heavy relaxation weighted his limbs. As he blinked away the last vestiges of sleep, the solidness of her in his arms and the steady rhythm of her breathing stopped him from stretching away the muscles stiff from resting.

At first, he'd thought he might be imagining it. Maybe dreaming the whole thing because he'd wanted her for so long. The steady rise and fall of her chest as she lay at peace—one breast revealed by the blanket he'd pulled over them—wiped away the possibility of his imagination fabricating the situation. They'd made love again, as he'd fantasized, but better, and she was with him.

Fast on the heels of him realizing she'd fulfilled his erotic plans came the knowledge that at some point she'd wake up. And then they'd need to talk.

Lowe had found an out, a way to undo their marriage as if it'd never happened and enable him to keep the shares—a text he'd received while she was sleeping. His father had written in a six-month clause into his paperwork, stating he'd need to stay married to Jeanie if he wanted the shares, but Lowe and his team managed a loophole. He'd have the shares within the week either way, and Jeanie could leave if she wanted.

Lowe found the loophole—after so long being unsuccessful—which awakened an unwelcome memory of Lowe warning Camden she'd be fair game if they ever split. Jealousy, unfamiliar and barbed, raced through him. Terror iced across his skin and raised goose bumps.

He couldn't lose her, not after what they'd shared. He cared for her; she wanted him. He needed to convince her to stay with him. They could be good together, they could be happy.

Her breath sped a little, and she curled closer to him and nuzzled at his neck. He shook as his body hardened, ready and willing to show her just how much he wanted her to stay and only held back by iron control. The nipple of her exposed breast came in contact with his chest and hardened to a puckered peak, further testing his resolve to stay still so he didn't wake her.

Unable to resist any longer, even knowing that her eyes opening meant they'd talk and it all might fall apart again, he wrapped his arms around her and curled his leg over her hip to pull her close. She sighed a little, her lips rubbed against his neck, and he cupped her head to keep her there.

Her hips moved, pushed against him, and he shuddered out a breath. He'd tried to go slow with her, afraid of asking her for more than she wanted to give, but even when he tried to make it good for her, she'd moved beneath him, demanding more.

Careful, he'd planned to be so careful with her, but she'd refused his caution and driven him faster. Soon he'd lost himself entirely to the feel of her moving with him and the sight of her face, tense with desire.

The overwhelming nature of his feelings for her should terrify him. It should leave him backing away, wanting to create space between them to ensure he wouldn't get more tangled than he could afford to be.

Instead, he settled more firmly around her, and she murmured in her sleep. When her head turned, he couldn't resist dropping a quick kiss on her lips, still swollen from their hours of loving.

Her eyes blinked open slowly, and a smile stretched her mouth before her eyes went wide, and she scrambled to pull the sheet over the bottom half of her face. "Hi," she mumbled from beneath the cover.

Not deterred, he nibbled at the sweet spot right behind her ear before whispering back, "Hi."

"I'll be right back." She scrambled out of the bed and pulled the sheet with her to hide her nudity. This, of course, pulled it off him, and she paused, head tilted at a comical angle. It seemed she considered his cock, which saluted her in response.

She shook her head and scuttled to the bathroom. When he heard the water running, he snuck out of the room to go to the next bedroom's bathroom to brush his teeth at mach speed and take care of his own toilette before making it back before she emerged.

When she finally peeked out of the bathroom, her hair had been brushed and her cheeks were pink. "I'm still naked."

"No you're not," he corrected. "You've got the sheet. I'm naked."

As if drawn by his words, her gaze landed again on his cock, still at attention. "Yes, you're naked."

He frowned. Although he'd feared their post-coital conversation, he'd not anticipated her being quite this nerve-packed. He stalked to the bathroom to loom over her as she peered at him around the corner of the door. "Are you coming out?"

"I'm still deciding," she answered.

He pulled the door partway open, then leaned on the doorframe to be closer to her. "Would you rather if I came in?"

"Um, probably we should talk."

He nodded. She finally opened the door the rest of the way and practically lunged into the room. He shook his head and followed her.

She picked up his shirt. He took it out of her hand and flung it across the room. She picked up her dress. He discarded it as well. "Will you stop doing that?" She tried to juggle the sheet and glared at him. He caught the end of it and tugged it free from her grasp. He couldn't help but grin at her outraged gasp.

"Nope. You're not going to need the clothes tonight. Or the sheet."

"Camden, we need to talk."

He nodded again. "We do."

"So what are you doing?"

His answer was to sweep her into his arms and kiss her until her arms twined around his neck and she sighed. He might not have all the answers. He might not know how to make her want to stay with him, but they could discuss all of it later. Once he told her, she might take the out.

But for tonight? She'd given herself to him. He was determined she wouldn't regret the choice, nor would she forget their time together. There were about twenty things he could think of he'd yet to teach his virginal bride about lovemaking...

No time like the present to get started on the list.

Chapter Twenty-Seven

She stretched and rolled to her side to find the other side of the bed empty. The pillow, though, still smelled like him, and she tugged it close to bury her face in it. All night, he'd tempted and teased her, not taking his own satisfaction—well, not until she expressed curiosity about his penis. Making a man as powerful and intelligent as Camden lose his breath and tremble in desire was heady stuff.

It turned out she could give as good as she got, in this arena at least. She wasn't half bad at it, after all. And he'd—

She couldn't even think of words to describe all the things they'd done. Her smile spread as memories of the night before rippled over her, causing little aftershocks of pleasure to clench the muscles between her legs and leave her belly full of butterflies.

He'd never tired of her, seeming just as thrilled by this part of their relationship as she couldn't help but be. They'd not talked, other than whispered demands and sighs of pleasure. Every time she'd thought they might talk, he'd teased another overwhelming orgasm from her well-used body, and she'd forgotten she'd planned to talk first.

Somehow, the idea of talking wasn't as scary now that she'd realized he loved her. He still hadn't said it, but the way he'd touched her? It wasn't just sex and a business arrangement.

But a new morning dawned, sunlight kissing their honeymoon suite, and she couldn't hide from the facts any longer. She'd made love to her husband—repeatedly—and she still didn't know what he wanted out of their pairing, not really, even if she could guess based on his actions he must feel something more than general caring for her.

It seemed beyond illogical for him to actually want to keep up the pretended marriage, not when it didn't serve any purpose she could glean if he didn't love her. It wasn't like her appearing on his arm brought him any additional acclaim or helped his business any. Not to mention they'd had sex—*repeatedly.*

Had she made a huge mistake? Was she just as bad as her mother, really, unable to think when it came to sex? He'd never once said he loved her, nor had he promised to make their vows into a real attempt at marriage, only agreed they could blend business with pleasure. Putting words to action, they'd had a *lot* of sex, and she'd woken up alone.

Probably that wasn't a good sign.

Fumbling her way out of the sheet she'd somehow tangled up in while she slept, she managed to make it to the bathroom. Finding her rumpled clothes—which he'd tossed after round one and right before round two—she dressed and ran her hand through her hair. Grabbing her cell phone off the nightstand, she fired off a text to Lori to check on Kaycee.

She's fine. I'm assuming you're still with Camden?;)

He popped around the corner, two mugs of coffee in hand and...humming. His face looked more relaxed than she'd ever seen it, the constant lines carved in it from exhaustion gone, and a smile that didn't look calculating curved his lips. She narrowed her eyes at him. "You look quite chipper."

"Surprisingly, you don't. You're thinking too hard. Quit giving me scrunchy face and drink some coffee." He ducked his head and slanted his lips across hers, and she melted into the kiss. Once she couldn't breathe right, he lifted his head again to smile down at her. "Good morning."

"Good morning," she sighed back at him.

Cupping the mug of coffee in her hands, she wondered how hard it would be to convince him to crawl right back into bed.

"So, last night you wanted to talk."

Since she'd been sipping the coffee, she swallowed a bigger gulp than she planned and burned her tongue. Once she'd choked for a second and shot him a glare, she managed, "Yes, I believe I tried to bring that up a few times."

"We have forever to talk. We're married, and I've explained that it suits me to stay that way." He shrugged, not looking concerned.

"Camden—"

"You, drink the coffee. I'll talk." He stroked his fingertips across her forehead, moving her hair to tuck it behind her ear. "I'm sorry."

"You're sorry?" She blinked at him, and a hundred

possible reasons for his apology flitted through her mind before the novelty of him apologizing caught up with the list. "For what, exactly?"

"I'm sorry I wasn't more careful with you. In my defense, I, well, kind of got caught up in the moment. I said things I shouldn't have said, but I wanted you. I have wanted you, for quite some time to be honest."

She believed him, having been swept away in the storm of emotion herself. "Okay."

"I don't regret being with you, just to be clear. I do regret the way I acted before we made it to the bedroom..." He trailed off, one brow arched and lips scrunched. "Let me just be blunt. I can't think of a flowery way to say, 'I was so damned turned on and I've wanted you for so long, I couldn't see straight, not to mention think in any kind of logical way, so I acted like an ass.'"

She smiled. "Um, me either. Or too. Whichever."

He dropped a kiss on her forehead.

She waited for him to add something, to admit he loved her.

She chewed on her lip and tilted her head. She finally met his blue-eyed gaze. "You want us to stay and keep things as they are...because we had sex. Like past the shares, just stay here indefinitely?"

"Yes." He looked relieved. "I didn't think you'd understand quite so easily."

She shook her head and put down the coffee. When her thoughts scrambled on top of one another, she reached for it again and took another gulp. "So we'd what? Be married in name, have sex, and everyone is happy? That works for you?"

He nodded.

"What happens when the attraction wears off? Then we're simply smiling strangers sharing a house?" She searched his face and hoped she'd see that he understood. That he'd admit he wanted that, too.

"We've discussed my feelings on that topic, Jeanie. I think being married is enough. It will offer you security. We don't have to be alone, we would have each other." He shrugged. "It removes all the usual lies couples tell each other that are eventually proved impossible and leads to breaking up. We could have the kind of relationship most people want, but don't know how to maintain."

"What if I'm not built like that? What if I need more than a roommate and lover? Maybe I can't work that way, can't turn off all my emotions like you can? What if I need love?"

"I want you to stay because you're my *wife*." His voice went a little hoarse, and his face looked serious. He cleared his throat and tried again, his expression modulated to a calm, and far more distant, mask. "You're safer here. Staying makes sense; it is the logical choice for you."

She stepped away from him. "I'll always cherish what you did for me and Kaycee, but…"

She trailed off.

She could walk away. She could collect Kaycee and move somewhere else. File for a divorce or annulment or whatever…and it would be a very safe choice, as she'd go on with her life as it had been before he swept into it with his fast talk and contracts.

Or she could gamble on the fact he didn't look like a man who was simply being logical. He looked like a man who cared very much what she thought. She could stick around, see if those budding emotions turned into love. She could wait him out, make him admit it.

In the meantime, she could show him how great having her as a wife would be.

She turned back to face him, then sat her mug on the nearby hall table before going up on tiptoes to slip her arms around his neck. The tension in his body didn't release as he waited for her verdict. Which got her thinking...*why today?*

Why was he pushing for her to commit to stay? It couldn't be just because they'd had sex. He wasn't a man led by emotions, hence the entire conversation up to that point.

"So, you want me to stay, but you haven't said why you're bringing it up. I've been here all week, after all, and you didn't bring any of this up until this morning."

If she'd thought his expression to be shuttered before, it snapped closed entirely at her words. An actual mask would have revealed more than his expression. "No, I didn't."

"What changed?"

He turned away from her, shoulders tense as he looked down the hallway toward the still open bedroom door. "They've found the loophole."

Her hand fluttered to her throat.

"I've told you, I care about you. We're good together."

She shook her head. "And I've told you, that's not enough. Not for me."

Maybe it would hurt her to go, but it was better she leave while she remembered he'd written the words on the wall clear enough for even her to read. He didn't love her, maybe couldn't love anyone, and only a fool would continue to live in an illusion so well built, she'd even begun to believe it.

She remembered, in vivid detail, the day before.

And then the *night* before.

She'd come on to him, ripped off her clothes, and thrown herself in his lap like some desperate and shameless thing...

His response?

He'd carried her to bed, dumped her on the mattress like a sack of unwanted potatoes, and left her. Then, later in the night, he'd made love to her, and she'd confessed she loved him. His response to that? He'd only told her thank you in response.

Thank you. Who in the hell said "thank you" when someone declared her love for you?

My husband, that's who.

Shaking her head, she refused to let tears spill. It wasn't like he didn't care about her. They'd been tired, had a long day, and she'd drank too much. Surely, with the light of day, he'd admit he felt the same way. He'd say the words...

"I love you," she whispered. He didn't answer, instead took her arm and led her to the kitchen of the suite.

"Look, I made coffee and breakfast. Nothing better for a bad head than a good, greasy breakfast. Rule number one, trust the hangover cure." He plated eggs, some toast, and bacon. She wasn't sure how she'd missed the bacon scent, but she'd been rather distracted by the coffee. Her nose, it seemed, had coffee-dar.

"I'm not hungry." As if to call her a liar, her stomach growled.

"Sure, you're not hungry. And I'm not rich. Now that we've lied once already this morning, let's eat, shall we?" His hand at her waist guided her to the table, and she considered the plate as she sat.

"It looks good." If she'd sounded startled, it wasn't her fault. He was a rich boy from rich blood. Cooking wasn't exactly a needed skill set.

"It tastes even better. Eat up. It will help, I promise." He sat across from her and began forking into his own breakfast.

"You're still in a suspiciously good mood." She considered his face as she said it and realized his tone was a big fat lie, bigger than any he'd ever told in her presence.

The tired expression dominated his face. Not just peeking through, completely revealed in his face, puffy from lack of sleep and dark circles carving deep lines under his brilliant blue eyes. His lips were pulled down, creating lines almost as deep as those under his eyes.

He looked tired. He looked defeated.

Which made no sense, of course. If anyone had a right to look damaged this morning, it was her.

She swallowed hard. She didn't like the sneak peek into his tortured soul. Eating gave her hands something to do. After a few bites—which were good, he hadn't lied about that—she lay her fork down.

"Camden, where do we go from here? You said we aren't getting divorced. You have your shares now, or must since you married just like your dad required. I'm not useful to you anymore and—"

She broke off, because her voice was about to break. She wasn't sure she wanted the answers she'd demanded. If she was honest with herself, she cared about him. He'd wiggled under her skin and…

Well, God knew she couldn't resist the feel of him, the temptation of him. She'd not been able to shake the memory of their stolen moments in the car or the kiss in the hall—

for some reasons, those stuck out. Maybe because he'd not been acting for anyone during those occasions. Making her believe—or rather, hope—he wanted her.

As more than an employee and a means to an end.

As...well...as a woman.

Then that night in the dark...when she'd come to him, and he'd held her. Her heart seemed to squeeze in her chest at the memory. When she'd woken, he gazed down at her, not looking as tired, but more open than she'd ever seen him. His whimsical smile as he'd whispered *Hello, you* and traced his hand across her cheek and into her hair left her shivering even in memory.

But the questions needed to be asked. "I'm not useful to you anymore. So, where do we go from here?"

"Well, I thought maybe later we could go on a boat tour. Maybe do the winery thing—I've heard they do tastings, and those are supposedly quite romantic. Very honeymoon variety stuff." He continued to eat his breakfast, his face cast down so she couldn't read his expression.

She'd told him she loved him, and he'd thanked her. He hadn't returned her sentiment, so maybe she was useful to him, but what did she need to be happy? She thought she'd be okay without love, even though her feelings for him were growing and the vows meant she'd be with him constantly, but in the cold light of day, she wasn't.

When he hadn't said he loved her, she'd felt so disappointed. She knew better now. She needed someone who loved her. "I can't do this."

As soon as the words slipped out, she longed to pull them back. To have unsaid them, or perhaps not thought them.

Her heart, as if to make up for the fear clogging it only a moment before, seemed to race double time in her chest and rattle against her ribs.

"Jeanie, if this is about sex—"

"No. Or mostly no...." She couldn't finish. Shame, an oily beast with sharp scales, slicked through her veins, cutting and leaving nasty residue where it passed.

"I think I've made it clear that I want you."

Wanting was a far cry from loving. He'd taught her important lessons in passion over the duration of their time together. Desire clawed, hot and demanding, not manufactured or easy to stop once it started. Desire hardened her nipples; left her breathless, aching, needing him to take the passion he wakened and turn it into something tense and fragile.

If he loved her, he would likely say something this morning. His hands would have shaken, just a little, like they did before he kissed her sometimes. Then his tongue would have thrust into her mouth, demanding her response, while his hands raced across her flesh. He would have made her cry out, like in the limo, bringing her to shaking orgasm, and he would have done it again and again until the edge of the continuous starvation for flesh found some kind of satiation.

He hadn't.

None of it. He'd made breakfast instead of saying anything or trying to touch her at all.

"You don't have to tell me you don't want me, Camden. Actions speak louder than words, isn't that the saying?" Reminding herself that for him it was only a business transaction didn't stop the growing ache in her chest. Maybe he'd enjoyed himself in the meantime, but it couldn't last. She tried to keep bitterness out of her tone, but she'd guarded herself against attachment, kept her heart safe for so long, knowing what damage love could do.

She'd guarded against it, avoided letting anyone close enough to hurt her like her mother hurt her dad—and her, to be honest. Her mother hurt her, betrayed her, and refused to really see past herself long enough to realize her daughter needed a mommy...

But no matter how much Jeanie guarded against love, it'd found a crack. It had snuck up while she wasn't watching and it'd bit her in the ass.

She loved him—arrogant mask, tired mask, lonely man walking the floors all night—she loved the wretched creature from the top of his dark head to the bottom of his feet.

Fuck.

She braced her hand on the doorframe, and then she caught sight of the rings. The perfect rings, the wedding set she would have picked if she'd looked a lifetime for it, and another cold slap of reality hit her.

He was her husband, and she loved him. She could shut up now. Take back the words she'd said and let him live the lie he'd so carefully crafted. She could be his wife, revel in the joy of his arms around her, smile for the press and the whole world would think she had everything.

Everyone, that is, except me. I'll know. I'll know it's the perfect lie, the happiest lie.

Her father...had he loved her mother like this? Knowing what she was, how she was, and not caring because, if he could have her, did it matter if she only faked it?

She had an equal part of him and her mother inside her. She could be Camden's wife. She could love him and never let him know she wasn't acting any more.

But it's not enough.

I know how that story ends.

I saw it, I watched him come home to her. I watched him turn a blind eye to the obvious signs that she cheated, that she used him, that he'd never make enough money or be enough or...

"I refuse that," she whispered to the beach.

"You said that already." She hadn't noticed he'd come to stand behind her, too lost in the game changing view of herself.

She turned, faced him, and knew what she had to do. "So, what happens next, Camden?"

"Well, according to all the books, once the handsome prince solves all the problems, he and the princess live happily ever after."

His attempt at humor fell flat, and she frowned at him. "You're no prince, and I'm not a princess—far from it. You married me; everyone saw it. The world knows I'm your bride. You can get your shares back, but you don't need me anymore other than on paper. Maybe it'd be better if I went on a vacation somewhere, just vanished for a while."

She gave him the words she needed him to say—pushed them at him so hard, she was sure he'd hear her thoughts just from the look in her eyes. Her very soul begged him to say them.

I do need you, Jeanie. I've fallen in love with you. Please don't leave me.

He didn't say any of the things she wanted to hear. Instead, he shrugged, mogul mask firmly in place on his exhausted face. "Well, we're on our honeymoon now, so—"

"I said you don't need me here now. I could go. I can walk out the door, and it won't change a thing. You'll still get everything you want. I'll still get paid. We'll both walk away from this with what we were promised when we started. Are you okay with that?"

She wished he'd say *No, stay*. Catch her hands or her face and hold her and admit he felt something, too. That it wasn't just her. That she wasn't the only one who fell into the trap of the lies and faked intimacy.

"It'd be lonely in the resort all by myself. Let's just forget you brought this up for now, table it for later, so we can enjoy ourselves and a much-deserved break from public life. It'll be fun. I promise. We can figure out beyond that as it happens, once we're back at the penthouse."

She shook her head, slowly. If she stayed, even for the day, she'd fall deeper under his spell and might never break free of it. She wanted so badly for him to be something he obviously wasn't. She wanted the act to be reality. The vacation *would* be fun. It would be thrilling and challenging, and she'd laugh harder than she'd ever laughed before she'd met him, she was sure of it.

It'd be wonderful.

So wonderful, maybe she could convince herself she saw signs of his real feelings. Maybe she'd have more moments like the limo and the darkness and the zoo to add to the list of reasons she knew he cared.

Even though he didn't. Not really.

"Take me home, Camden. I'll go pack." She slid between him and the wall, not even noticing he'd come into her personal space because she'd become accustomed to that part of his personality. But she didn't touch him.

She might not be able to walk away if she touched him.

She made it to her room without letting a single tear fall. Her hangover raged, her stomach roiled, and her heart broke. She wouldn't cry, though.

She pulled off her wedding rings and left them on the bedside table so she could shower without worrying about them. That'd be all she needed to top off her morning—losing rings worth more than a year's worth of salaries.

She ran through her shower on autopilot. She dressed and avoided looking at her reflection. If she saw herself, acknowledged what she was doing, she might not be able to do it.

She grabbed her bag headed outside as her phone dinged an incoming text.

She could see Camden, out on the sand, considering the waves. Her heart ached, and she longed to go to him…to wrap her arms around him and let her life go to the promise of happily ever after. The door closed behind her with a very final-sounding *click*.

"I'll meet you at the car," she called out to him. He glanced back toward her and nodded, but she didn't wait for him to catch up, instead heading for the car. The walk through the hotel felt longer by daylight, as if the night shrunk the distance because she'd headed towards a dream, while by morning she walked away from it.

She could go on without him.

Even if the idea of doing it left her so empty and more alone than she could ever remember feeling. Like someone filled her heart with shards of glass so every breath hurt, but it would get better.

It had to.

Chapter Twenty-Eight

Two days had passed since they'd left their pseudo-honeymoon to resume relative normalcy. Neither spoke a word about what conspired on the disaster of a trip. Instead, Camden just barked out orders to the staff and spent most of his time closed in his office.

She developed a pattern of sorts, always knowing he wasn't far away but that a gulf separated them. She woke up in the morning, played with Kaycee, worked with her on letters and numbers, gave her a bath, and went to bed.

Sometimes her phone beeped with an email, listing the appropriate clothing and where they were going. Without a word, she'd dress, then find her husband waiting by the bank of elevators, generally looking at his watch. No words were spoken as they traveled to whatever event. Once there, they went through the motions. She never met his eyes, practically memorizing how to look at him and focus only on his collar.

The kisses he'd peppered through their every interaction

prior to the wedding were replaced with his hand at her waist or neck, and even those touches were given without the slightest personal connection.

Constantly, she battled tears, aching for what they'd had and how easily it'd slipped away. Her smile stayed pasted in place, her responses stayed polite, and no one seemed to notice the strain of her performance. She did her job, exactly, to the letter accomplishing what he'd paid her to be.

She didn't sleep the nights away, instead imagined him, only a few rooms away, and stared out the window at the night as it passed below. She imagined, in those late hours, that they were perhaps the only two people in the city awake—staring into the darkness and yet unable to see each other across the chasm of class and pain which spanned between them. On the upside, being tired helped the days blur together and almost gave her something to focus on other than the empty hole in her chest where her heart used to live.

Almost.

It shouldn't surprise her that he avoided her unless cameras loomed. When they did, his smiling mask matched the one she'd been perfecting, and they presented exactly what the public expected—the happy couple.

Even though she couldn't get him out of her head.

She released the curtain she'd been holding and pulled out her phone as it beeped. She thumbed it unlocked, saw the email from Camden James, and opened it on a sigh.

Business casual, the missive advised, and she glanced down at the salmon colored dress fastened with a leather belt. If she simply slipped into a pair of low heels, what she wore already would work. She snagged the shoes and her purse, then reapplied her lip-gloss before heading out to the bank of elevators.

He stood, in designer jeans and a steel colored shirt, only the vibrancy of one of his pink ties breaking up the almost stark image of important man waiting impatiently. "Ready?" he asked.

She nodded. Lately, it seemed better if she just didn't speak. Once they were in his car, she carefully kept her posture correct, feet off the dash, everything almost painfully polite.

He parked in front of the art museum, and a valet opened her door. She waited for Camden to exit the car, then took his offered arm. Her smile might have been brittle, but looking around at the other wealthy and elitist figures filling the gallery at the top of the stairs, she realized most of them probably wore masks, too. Perhaps that was how no one saw through their lies.

Everyone lied.

In moments, someone swept Camden into conversation, and Jeanie made small talk with a woman she'd met at other such events. She couldn't recall the name, but she'd found it didn't matter at these engagements. Someone would let the name of the other speaker drop in conversation, and she could bluff until then.

Actually, she was getting pretty good at living the lies.

A hand touched her side. She jolted and looked up at Lowe. Still model-handsome, the other man wasn't wearing a mask. He looked concerned.

"Jeanie, do you have a moment?"

She made excuses to exit her prior conversation, then trailed after him as he led her to an alcove for a bit of privacy.

"Are you okay?" he asked without further ado.

Her fake smile withered under his knowing look. "I'm fine. Why would you ask?"

"Look, Jeanie." He leaned close and lowered his voice so only she could hear him. "He told you about the loophole, right? I hadn't heard if you wanted to go ahead with it, although it seemed safe to assume you'd worked out your issues together. I don't know what happened, but—"

"Take your hands off my wife." Camden's voice snapped with fury, more emotion than she'd heard from him for days. Jeanie blinked at him in surprise, but Lowe found his voice first.

"Look, Cam—"

But he hadn't released her, so Camden went into motion and shoved Lowe away. "I said don't touch her."

Lowe raised his hands and brows, then strode away in obvious annoyance.

Jeanie's own anger riled at the interaction, and she faced off with her husband. "That was really uncalled for. What, I'm not allowed to talk to—"

"If it is a man in your bed you're looking for, wife, I'm happy to fulfill my husbandly duty."

White-hot rage bathed her, and flames of heat rose up her neck and seemed to shoot out her mouth as words. "You arrogant... He was talking to me—something you can't be bothered to do, and you tell him off and then insult us both?" She thumped his chest again, then backed him into a wall. "How dare you?"

He licked his lips, looking like some seductive sex demon intent on devouring her right there in the art museum. "You'd be amazed what I'd dare, Jeanie."

"I don't know what this is all about, but all he wanted was to find out what I wanted to do about the loophole. He was doing his job, Camden, as you hired him to do."

He blinked at her, not seeming even a little less angry. "So he took you aside alone to ask? So what did you tell him?"

"Nothing. You interrupted. However, I'll tell you what I think…I need some time. I want to think things through."

"Jeanie—"

But she was tired of his emotional constipation, his fast talking, and his arrogance. She was tired of feeling like she saw something more to him only to have his words confirm it'd been a glittering lie. "I said I need some time to think. Don't try to contact me, because I'm not going to answer. I'll let you know what I decide when I know."

With that, she turned her back on her husband and went to collect her child from his lovely tower of empty promises.

Chapter Twenty-Nine

He rubbed his hand across the stubble on his face, then rolled his neck to loosen the muscles. He didn't know where she'd gone.

Any logical person would have realized he'd offered her all that he had. It wasn't his fault he wasn't foolish enough to believe in love, and really, her believing could be labeled childish. Most women would have jumped at his offer — security, sexual compatibility, and wealth without the unstable foundation of romantic notions cluttering the marriage. He'd proved they were good together.

But she'd left. No explanation beyond words they'd both spoken in the heat of anger. And she'd ignored his calls as she'd promised, even as he damned himself for being an idiot for trying. If she refused to see reason, why should he bother to continue the conversation?

But he did call. And she didn't answer.

His exhausted brain seemed unwilling to whir to life, to

come up with answers. Dealing with her made no sense, so how could he hope to find explanations for her irrational behavior? Late in the night, he found himself walking through her rooms—the toys he'd bought for Kaycee still littered the floor like ghosts of the child lingering to haunt him.

Probably it was for the best. He knew he'd likely make a poor father anyway. Playacting at husband and father with them had been an amusing way to pass time, and it had served a purpose, but he could go back to his life as it had been before they'd basically invaded and thrown everything topsy-turvy.

Once inside Jeanie's room, he moved to her bed and lay on his back. The ceiling in her bedroom was identical to his own, but her sheets still carried the remnants of her scent. More ghosts, as if he needed them, but these ones he could easily exorcise. One visit from the maids, and he could erase their presence from his rooms if not from his mind.

The glitter on the bedside table caught his eye, and he sat up so fast that he had to blink past a wave of vertigo. He focused on the two rings neatly resting next to the lamp.

What kind of woman left behind rings like those? Surely even Jeanie realized he'd practically shoved a fortune on her finger. If she'd taken them and sold them, she and Kaycee could live in relative comfort for the rest of her days. But she'd left them behind, discarded them—discarded *him*— because he wasn't enough.

Which he'd known.

He picked the rings up, cupped them in his hand, and stared at the proof she'd gone and didn't intend to come back. But they proved more than her absence…

They proved she might not be like every other woman he'd met. She wasn't a fool, since he knew she recognized the monetary value of the baubles. It simply hadn't mattered to her.

Perhaps not all women lied and focused on wealth. Perhaps she truly was the rarest gem—a woman more concerned with emotional depth than wallet depth.

And she'd left him, really left him, not just left their home.

He gathered the rings and held them to his chest. He felt broken in a way he didn't know how to cure. He'd offered her everything he had. He'd told her he cared, cherished her body.

But it—he—wasn't enough.

His phone beeped, and he thumbed it awake. *Your wife texted me. Gave me the go ahead to proceed with the loophole.*

Lowe. She'd left him...for Lowe. Maybe she hadn't planned it that way, but Lowe could offer her the one thing Camden couldn't. Hadn't Tasha said it clearly only weeks before? Lowe was the kind of man who had something Camden didn't. Lowe could love her, could believe in all the emotional mumbo jumbo, while Camden couldn't pretend...

The betrayal should have been expected. Everyone left eventually.

He tossed the phone as hard as he could throw it, then carried the rings back to his rooms and stood in the bay windows. Like every other night, the city lay beneath his so called lair—money changing hands, people living and dying, and him far above, removed from all of it. Never part of the pulse, always alone.

Except he hadn't been alone. Not while Jeanie was with

him.

She'd filled up the darkness, made him feel like he was part of something.

And he'd basically shoved her away because he was afraid.

Always afraid, the poor little rich kid. Born with a silver spoon and the knowledge that the only thing loveable about him was the number of zeroes in his bank account. Maybe he was just like his dad after all; he'd simply deluded himself into believing otherwise.

Because when it mattered? He hadn't been enough, either.

He moved to his desk, picked up the phone there, and dialed. He tapped his fingertips on the desk and fidgeted until he heard his best friend answer.

"Hey, did she say anything else?" Camden asked.

"Why would she? I thought 'proceed with the loophole' was rather clear, myself." Lowe's tone didn't give him an iota of sympathy, and Camden's lips tightened in repressed frustration.

"So does this mean you're going through with your earlier threat? If she's single, then she's fair game?" He wished he could resist asking, but he felt like a raw nerve, as if everything he'd worked his whole life to hide was suddenly exposed and vulnerable.

Lowe's laugh filled his ear, but he didn't answer it. Finally, his friend asked softly, "Do you really think I'd go after the one woman who loves my friend? Because that'd be a rather dick move on my part, and I honestly believed you thought better of me after all these years."

Camden swallowed hard and rubbed his face with one

hand. "That wasn't meant as a slur against you, Lowe. I mean, I get it."

"Do you get it, Cam? Because it sure as hell sounds like you don't."

"What I meant was I get why you'd want to. She's…" He trailed off, thinking of everything Jeanie was. If he believed in things like love…

Maybe that was the core, the root of the problem. Maybe he'd been so convinced that he didn't believe in love, he'd missed it entirely when he stumbled across the kind of thing people wrote poetry about. His feelings for her were more than something so simple as love, though. He needed her. He couldn't imagine going through the rest of his life as he'd lived before—everything had been so empty and meaningless before she stormed into his life and changed him.

"I love her, Lowe."

Camden could almost hear the smile in Lowe's words. "For a genius, you're kind of slow, brother. Now, instead of telling me, have you mentioned that very important fact to her?"

Chapter Thirty

When Kaycee had been a baby, there'd been many nights Jeanie only managed a couple of hours rest, because infants didn't sleep for long. Time, during that period, seemed to stretch out because of her exhaustion. She'd been sure, back then, her experience explained why they measured babies' ages in months—because a month became a very long stretch if the parent wasn't sleeping.

Yet the week since she'd been parted with Camden seemed longer than any she'd ever survived in the past, more like a year, and all of it filled with her thinking in circles and always coming back to one truth. She loved him.

She'd probably always love him.

He'd changed her, inside and outside. Even her choice of dress morphed because of her time with him. Instead of jeans and an old tee shirt, her previous wardrobe of choice for a day off work, she'd worn a flirty skirt that swished around her legs in a pleasing way coupled with a soft blousy shirt. It turned out she liked the dollop of femininity she experienced when she wore soft fabrics against her skin. It granted a certain level of confidence, and she'd need every iota of added confidence she could find if she hoped to accomplish what she'd planned.

The bank of elevators loomed, and she stopped before the doors, remembering her first trip up to his private world. In an almost ironic parallel, a group of banker-looking people gathered around her, waiting for their ride up. She almost smiled at the memory of that fateful day. It seemed so long ago, but then she'd been a different person at that point.

The doors opened, and she stepped inside. In moments, she was surrounded by the banker-types, so she stared at the gleaming brass. The blurry reflection in the polished metal didn't look much like the frizzy haired girl who'd tried to save her job. Her stomach still flipped with a blend of panic and dread, only barely spiced with dregs of hope, but her mask of composure didn't reveal it—also thanks to practicing hiding what she felt when she'd been with Camden.

A slight shift in the floor signaled they'd arrived, then the doors swished open. Her heart raced as she lifted her chin, but she didn't need the illusion of the group to get where she was going.

The marbled floor, slick under her low heels, led into a conference room to the left and an office on the right. The men filed in to the left, and she smiled at the guy in front of her when he turned and caught sight of her. If she was correct, it might have been the same man who held the chair out for her on the day she'd met Camden. She shook head at her own reminiscing and turned the knob on the office, not bothering to knock. She breezed past the secretary and inside, to where Lowe waited.

"Lowe, you said you were going to finalize the paperwork, but I wanted to talk to you." Facing him, actually seeing his model-perfect features again, brought it all back in a way that squeezed her heart. She would rather have talked to Camden, but she'd decided this route would be the best way to gain the Penthouse Prince's attention. Surely, as a dedicated businessman, he'd appreciate her using legalities rather than an emotional display to make her point.

"Jeanie, how have you been? I've been worried, but I didn't want to overstep…" His dark brows initially startled upward at her barging in, but now quickly scrunched in concern. He came around the desk, slung an arm around her shoulders, and pulled her farther into the office. He shoved the door closed. "What did you want to talk about?"

She relaxed into his embrace for a second, then sucked in a jagged breath. "About the paperwork—"

A soft knock snared her attention, but the visitor didn't wait to be called in. The door opened and revealed Camden pushing past Lowe's secretary. Behind him, she could see the boardroom door also stood open, and the men inside peered curiously across the hall. His father stood at the head of the table, just visible from her vantage. The older man didn't look pleased to see her.

For a moment, all the air seemed to be sucked from the room, suspending Jeanie in a vacuum. Camden looked so good, so damned perfect, and she wanted to run to him. To ask him if he'd missed her, thought of her, to see if he smelled the same.

To confess she loved him. And if he didn't love her? It

didn't matter. She'd take his caring, if that was all he had to offer, so long as it meant she could be with him.

She didn't say any of it. Emotions clogged her throat to the point that she couldn't breathe past the ball of them no matter how many times she swallowed. She'd already been down that road. Now she knew better.

"Hey, Lowe, I thought I saw—" Camden's words snapped to a halt when his cobalt gaze rested on her. Like clouds chased across the sky by fast winds, expressions flitted across his face while she watched. "You're here." He practically whispered the words, yet each one seemed to echo in her mind with a jarring resonance.

She couldn't seem to slow her heart. Adrenaline pumped through her system with each beat and left her restless. She searched for the words that would answer him without admitting he'd hurt her. Her mind seemed trapped on a loop, repeating their time together until she viewed everything differently.

Even when he'd acted as if what they shared didn't matter, how many times had she seen his hands tightened to fists as if to resist touching her? Then, when he had touched her, the fine tremors that had shaken his fingertips, as if he were touching something precious?

He might not ever call it love, but she'd had time to decide which mattered more—a man willing to say he loved her or one who showed it in a hundred ways but couldn't say the words.

He slid into motion first, crossing the floor to stand in front of her. Murmurs from behind him suggested the members of the board and his father hadn't stayed in the boardroom and instead had come out to see the rest of the show.

She opened her mouth, sure she'd find the right words this time.

He held up a single hand. His gaze darted behind him, then focused on her. "Can you give me a second?" he asked.

She blinked, startled, and then nodded jerkily. Of all the things she'd imagined he might say when they were face to face again, him asking for a second and basically putting her off hadn't been a possibility.

He loosened his tie, seemed to brace himself before facing the men behind him. "Dad, I'm going to be honest and admit the whole relationship with Jeanie was faked. I hired her to pretend to be my fiancée when I heard Tasha got caught cheating in Cannes."

"I knew it," his father practically crowed.

"That said?" Camden continued, his brow arched and posture lacking any defeat. "I've never believed in love, so there wasn't even a possibility I'd have a real marriage when I hired her. You were right about me, everyone was. You paraded women in and out of my life, I've always felt that you killed my mother, and I've been entirely sure I wasn't loveable, if such an emotion did exist. I was honestly sure love was a lie—something people used to explain biological and economical needs—and everything I saw proved me right."

Jeanie slumped a little, any pretended composure dragging under the weight of his declarations.

"I've made it clear…" Camden paused and scanned the gathering employees and onlookers, "that I didn't believe in love, and that anyone who claimed to was fooling themselves. So, yes, Dad, you were right. My engagement to Jeanie was fake, and my marriage was a lie. However, you're a very intelligent man, Dad, so I'm sure you've noticed I used the past tense. You *were* right about me. My marriage *was* fake. But now you're wrong."

His father grumbled, but Jeanie didn't look at him, too intent to hear what Camden might say next.

"At first, when I saw Jeanie, something clicked—I knew I had to convince her to pretend to be my fiancée. As time passed, I realized I loved her smile, the way she snarls at me, even her perfect moral compass—especially compared to my obviously broken one. I loved her smell, the way her hair looked in sunlight, and the way her eyes turned all mysterious at night. She saw me, really saw me, when no one else ever bothered to try. Little things, really, yet they built up."

Her hand seemed to move of its own volition, covering her mouth as if she could hold in the emotions threatening to spill out. *Could he mean…?*

When he faced her, her tears erupted, streaming down her face. Even in front of his father and the members of the board, his mogul mask was gone. The tired man, the tender one, gazed at her—exposed to the room and vulnerable. "So, I've realized you're wrong, Dad. About me, about what I want out of life, and more importantly about what matters most."

With a hiccup of a sob, her vision blurred. She scrubbed her hands against her eyes, not caring if she trashed her mascara, and blinked fast to clear her eyes.

He reached for her hand, and she gave it to him, stunned when he dropped to one knee. "I thought you said if you ever knelt, I'd be the one begging," she managed.

"I didn't do this right the first time, so I'm trying again."

"Camden—" she began.

He touched a fingertip to her lips. "Shh. Let me do this right."

She couldn't speak, hoping he might say the words she'd longed to hear.

He shrugged. "It turns out I'm not always right. I've missed you. My life has been empty without you. I didn't think I believed in love, and even if I had? I felt really certain I didn't deserve you. You should have someone better, someone not as stubborn and maybe someone who isn't as blind as I've been." He looked down and then glanced past her toward Lowe's office. "But dammit, I'm selfish, and I don't want to lose you, even if you do deserve better. Will you marry me? In fact, not pretend, and be my wife, not the woman playing the part?"

She knelt next to him, but he hadn't released her hand. "Cam—"

"Look, Jeanie, you left these behind, and I've kept them on my desk since you left. I get that I can't buy your love and that I'm probably going to find new ways to screw things up. I get that I should have said all that instead of telling you I cared, but I didn't. I can't change any of that, but I love you, dammit. And you said that would be enough."

He squeezed her fingertips, and she opened her mouth to answer, but he interrupted her again. "Besides, I tried giving you everything I thought any woman would want. I made sure Kaycee was safe, planned everything and nothing went right. I tried everything except this—I love you. I don't care why you stay with me, just don't leave."

She clamped her hand over his mouth and snickered. "If

you'd shut up, I could answer you. You don't have to ask me to marry you, Penthouse Prince, because I'm already your wife. I wasn't going to let you go. I love you, and my father always said that anything worth having is worth fighting for." He leaned closer, and she met his lips in a quick brush before adding, "And I think you're worth fighting for. I love you, Camden James."

Chapter Thirty-One

He hadn't planned to propose in his offices, hadn't planned to declare how he felt in front of his father, but it brought him a strange sense of peace to have done so. He'd looked at people who believed in love, who used that four-letter word, as weaker. It turned out that in practice, saying it gave him strength. He'd proclaim it on the cover of *People* magazine if she required it, because loving her could easily be called the best thing he'd ever done.

When she said she found him worth fighting for, though, he wished they'd had a bit more privacy. Although slanting his lips across hers—the taste of her sweeter than water after being trapped in a desert—could never be considered less than satisfying, the cheers that erupted reminded him they weren't alone. "Come home with me, wife," he whispered.

Her lip stuck out in a pout. "We are home, or one floor down anyway. You live in your office, rich kid."

"Good point," he agreed. With her lip sticking out that

way, he remembered their first meeting and his curiosity over how her mouth would taste. Now that he knew, for a fact, it tasted wonderful, his body stirred to life. He scooped her into his arms and glanced over his shoulder. "I'm taking the rest of the day off, so hold my calls." The cheer roared back to life, muted as the elevator doors closed behind them.

Her eyes were still a bit puffy from crying, but her smile lit up parts of him he hadn't realized were dark. "Oh, you think you're clever, Mr. James."

"I know I'm clever."

The doors whispered open, and he strode to his rooms and headed for the sitting room facing the bay windows. He put her on her feet, then turned to lock the door.

He led her to the seat where she'd spent the night in his arms. He sat and carefully replaced her wedding rings on her finger. Her soft sigh was a balm.

He nodded, satisfied to see the rings back where they belonged, then tugged her off balance from her elegant heels so she landed in his lap, an exotic-scented bundle of woman he couldn't seem to get enough of.

"That's better. I wanted to be alone with you. I'd come up with all these plans...but then I saw you and decided it would be now, here. I hope you don't mind that I didn't get to give you the grand romantic gesture I owed you."

Her fingers toyed with his hair, and she relaxed into his embrace. "Did you have to wait a whole week...?" She trailed off and met his gaze with her emerald one.

He pinched her ass, and he was pleased to see her squirm. "Hey, you left me, not the other way around."

The glint in her eye warned him before her nails dug into his scalp, and she moved to straddle him rather than sit across his legs. "I didn't leave you—you've haunted me every moment." A swivel of her hips made his chair squeak as she rubbed against his rock hard cock, and his breath stuttered out on a sigh. "I've missed you," she confessed, voice breaking a little.

He slid one hand up her waist and toyed with one nipple until it tightened sufficiently to poke out visibly beneath her bra and silky blouse. More interested in her eyes, he watched as they glazed in passion. He could spend the rest of his life simply watching her emotions drift like clouds across her expressive face.

He sucked one of her nipples into his mouth, and his tongue dampened her blouse to the point that he could see the dusky skin peeking through her lace demi cut. He leaned back and considered his handiwork. "I've missed you, too, and I've been putting a lot of thought into ways we can make this work. I told you I didn't deserve you, and I don't, but I'm going to do my best to make you happy, Jeanie."

She watched him closely as she streaked kisses over his chest. "I've been thinking quite a bit, too. I don't want to be one of those rich wives who just sits around all day getting bits buffed and waxed. I'm going to deserve you, too, since I think you're a lot more special than you give yourself credit for being."

"What do you want to do?" He freed the buttons on her blouse and pushed it from her shoulders. "Although I'll happily buff and wax you all day if you change your mind."

"Well, I've always been good with numbers, which means I could do something in accounting—Oh." As he tugged the bra down so he could give the hardened nipples more attention, she sighed, and her hips shifted again. "I'm not eliminating accounting entirely, but I think I want to do something to help children, if that doesn't sound too ridiculous."

"Doesn't sound ridiculous at all." It seemed he'd craved just the sight of her. The taste and feel of her fried his ability to think. The thread of the conversation slid away as he focused on her reactions, not pleased until her thighs trembled around him and she cried out her building need. Her hands became frantic, as if his starving hunger for her was contagious and she'd been infected by proximity.

His eager bride soon helped him strip her and they joined in desperation.

Her cries became words. "Camden. God, I love you."

"And I love you. I'm sorry I didn't tell you sooner. I love you, so damned much." As they raced toward the peak of tension, he realized she'd given him the greatest gift he'd ever received. Her. His only remaining task was making up to her all the moments she should have had. Luckily, he had a lifetime to make up for his mistakes.

Epilogue

The morning of her vow renewal ceremony—or real wedding, as she'd come to think of it—dawned with a storm blowing in. Camden fluttered around, frustrated because, yet again...

"I've planned the perfect romantic scene, and it's going to shit."

Jeanie didn't get concerned. One hand rested on the glass as she looked out on the beach and watched nature throw a tantrum. She knew it would be perfect because no storm had the power to ruin this day. After all, she was marrying her handsome prince.

When the clouds finally broke up a little and the rain stopped, she lifted her skirt and walked out onto the sand. The wind caught her hair, tangling it, and the sand stuck to her dress where it dragged behind her. The sun hung low in the sky and would set soon, the storm delaying the time of their ceremony by a couple hours from when they planned to say their vows.

Instead of the original plan, she got to be on the beach at sunset.

"We're not going to get any decent pictures." The wry twist of Camden's lips didn't fool her. She understood most of his worrying was because he wanted this to be a magical moment for her.

"Quit worrying. It's perfect. We don't need pictures. I'm never going to forget this, are you?" He reached for her hand, and she squeezed their fingers together before pushing him away. "Go, be a groom. You're supposed to stand over there."

The minister waited, book in hand, a serene look on her face.

Camden's dad came up behind her. He cleared his throat, and she turned to look at him. He was a jerk, a manipulator, and he was far from perfect, but his son's choices seemed to have made him rethink his own life. He'd been present, a first according to Camden, and seemed to be trying to get to know his son. It didn't hurt that he adored Kaycee, frustrating Camden with the easy affection he shared with the child—a direct opposite of Camden's distant and cold childhood. Both men were learning to love, lessons no one picked up overnight.

Lori snuck up behind the rich old man and pinched his butt as she passed to move to her position near the minister. Jeanie choked down a chuckle as the man adjusted his tie and collected his composure. "I meant to ask this sooner, but, well, I wasn't sure how to broach the topic—"

"Might want to speed this up a bit. My husband looks antsy." She looked away from her husband, who faced them, arms crossed, waiting for her to cross the beach to his side.

"Not to rush you, but you know how he gets."

The older man cleared his throat again and spoke softly. "I'm ever grateful for what you've done for my son. Since your father isn't here to give you away, would you like me to do the honor? And I mean that, it would truly be my honor to give you to my son in marriage."

She knew the words cost him, but she still couldn't say yes. "Thank you, really. It means a lot to me, and I'm honored you asked. This time? I *want* to give myself to him. I hope you're not offended—"

He kissed her cheek. "Thank you for letting me be here for this."

She nodded, and he left her side to stand near his son. They couldn't erase years of mistakes overnight, but Camden proved people could change if it mattered to them. Maybe his father would change, too.

She turned back to the hotel and held out her hand. Kaycee raced to her side. "Mommy, my flowers are all soggy." The pout to her lips echoed the whine in the child's voice.

Bending down, not concerned with the sand and her dress, Jeanie kissed both her cheeks and smoothed her hair. "You look beautiful. Perfect. Thank you for being here with me, baby girl."

Kaycee's lightning fast grin mimicked Camden's so perfectly, Jeanie swallowed back a laugh. "I get to stay up late tonight and have pop, right? Because it's a special occasion."

Jeanie stood and touched her back. "It's a very special occasion so, yes, you can stay up late and have pop. Go on up. It's your turn to walk down the aisle."

Skipping, Kaycee tossed globs of wet flower petals in

wads on the beach. Jeanie chewed the inside of her cheek to keep from laughing at the less than picture-perfect image. By the time she'd made it to Lori, scrunching her feet in the sand the whole way, the grit stuck to her ankles, making her feet and lower legs look dirty.

Jeanie grinned. This wedding was far more her style than the first ceremony—more real.

Wet beach, storm-tossed skies, and the rumble of thunder in the distance didn't detract from the far off sound of steel drums and the sight of the man she loved waiting to yet again promise to love her for the rest of their days.

As she smiled at him, his face cleared of worry like clouds parting to reveal the light. His outstretched hand beckoned her to join him. The cool sand under her feet and the breeze blowing across her skin soothed her, and she imagined the wind carried her father, checking in on his little girl as she again married the man of her dreams.

She paused, closing her eyes, and whispered, "Daddy, I found a really, really good man, and I'm really, really happy."

None of the worries or fears that plagued their first wedding day even touched the edges of her soul this time. Secure in her choice, she sighed in peace.

Leaving the past behind, she stepped into the future and took Camden's hand. He didn't stand on ceremony, instead pulled her into the circle of his arms.

He said his vows, and she repeated hers, never once looking away from his clear, blue gaze. She probably looked silly, standing there grinning up at him like a loon, but she didn't care.

She'd never been quite so happy.

Like their other wedding, he kissed her until she felt a

little dizzy, and then music rippled over the beach. He held her close, and she whispered in his ear, "*Marry Me*? Is this our song now? They played this at the first wedding…"

"I picked it both times. I might not have been able to find the words to tell you, but my heart knew what my brain refused to understand."

She stroked his jaw. "You picked the song? I just thought—"

"I picked it. Shh, now's not the time for talking. Let me hold you." He tucked her close to his chest, and his lips grazed her earlobe and sent shivers of need trembling through her. For the first time, she really listened to the lyrics of the slightly familiar song she'd disregarded the last two times he'd played it for her.

When the singer sang, "*Marry me…today and every day*," she sighed and blinked back tears. "Oh, Camden."

His slight nod was his only acknowledgement until he sang along with a bit of the song, right against her ear. "*Together can never be close enough for me to feel like I am close enough to you. You wear white and I'll wear out the words 'I love you' and 'you're beautiful.'*"

She turned her head, kissed her husband, and fell into the wonder of him, no concern about whether or not he'd catch her. "Thank you. I'm sorry I didn't hear it sooner."

"I think you heard it at just the right moment." They rubbed their noses together, and he grinned down at her as Lori, his father, and Kaycee broke into applause. "Promise me you'll always be happy by my side?"

"Nope." She bit his bottom lip, then pulled back before he could deepen the kiss. "But I promise to always be *by* your side."

"Thanks for taking a risk on a man who proposed within seconds of meeting you," he replied.

"Thanks for proposing to a woman on a mission to save her job." For a few moments, she simply enjoyed the feel of him against her. Then the first drops of rain landed on her, and she looked up to see the storm clouds had built back up while they'd said the words that linked their lives.

Kaycee squealed, and Lori grabbed her hand and waved at them before racing back to the hotel. Camden's father, far more proper, strode with a determined gait until he reached the safety of the porch then turned and waved. The minister was close behind him and closed the glass doors on the storm.

Camden didn't release her, and she didn't move away from him. She felt his heartbeat under her hand. Within moments, the full deluge poured on them and water ran in fast tracks down her cheeks. "So, we've got a private bungalow tonight?"

He licked the moisture off her cheek, igniting a thousand tiny fires of desire. "Yes, I specifically asked for an even bigger bed this time." Knowing why she asked, he didn't ask her permission before scooping her off her feet and setting off into the storm.

"You're carrying me?" Not that she minded. She could work on the buttons of his shirt and nibble kisses up his neck while they moved. "We're back to knight with raging hard on?"

"Yes, Mrs. James, I'm carrying you."

"You had better not dump me in the bed like a sack of unwanted potatoes and sit in the living room brooding all night like you did on our first honeymoon." She bit his earlobe before laughing.

"Oh, Mrs. James, I won't be sleeping a wink tonight, but I won't be brooding, either." The sexual promise in his voice further heated her blood, and she squirmed as he fumbled with the door and hauled her inside. He kicked it closed and continued onward, his destination clear.

"Look, if you're planning on keeping me up all night, I have stipulations."

He raised one brow and released her to slide down his body. "Should I call Lowe? If there's a contract, he wants to see it before I sign." He sighed heavily as he worked on divesting her of her wet and sandy gown. "You see, not too awful long ago, I wrote up this contract and came out of the whole deal with a wife. He thinks I make rash decisions."

"Hmm, we probably don't have to call Lowe." Glancing back at the bed, she giggled. "Lover, that's not a bed. That's a room with a duvet. Where on earth did you find a bed that big?"

"Perks of being really, really rich. If you want something, someone somewhere is selling it." His hands trailed over her skin, warming her rain-cooled flesh to volcanic temperatures between one heartbeat and the next. "Did I ever tell you the story of how I bought my bride?"

Her pulse raced, and her breath panted out, her desire for him never far from the surface. "Nah, but I don't want to hear it tonight."

"No?" His brow quirked. Then his tone changed from joking to serious, and his eyes locked on hers. "I love you so much."

"Love you, too. But I still don't want to hear your story." She stroked her hand down his jaw-line before trailing lower, then whispered, "Tonight, we start working on living happily ever after. Haven't you heard? No one ever tells that part of the story."

He lifted her and pulled her legs around his waist. "Can you think of a better way to spend our honeymoon? I mean, if I'm not brooding and you're not drunk and we don't tell stories?"

She didn't answer. She simply smiled, kissed her prince, and started working on the happily ever after.

Did you love this Indulgence? Check out more of our category romance titles at www.entangledpublishing.com/category/indulgence/

And for exclusive sneak peeks at our upcoming books, excerpts, contests, chats with our authors and editors, and more…

Be sure to like us on Facebook

Follow us on Twitter

Acknowledgements

A special thanks to my adopted fam—Shell, Jfab, Ma, and Dad. I really don't know what I'd do without you. Shell, without you taking me to see that movie which had the one-minute clip that inspired me? There would be no Camden James, so thank you. Thanks to my fabulous crit partners—Heather Long, Saranna DeWylde, and Rebecca Royce on this book. Jeanie, I named the heroine after you, so much love to ya. Xoxo to my genetic fam. I don't want to forget to mention all the family that doesn't have to be—the ones who aren't related by blood, but love me anyway—Ashleys, Schommers, Browns and others. You know who ya are. And thanks to my profs and fellow students at college cuz you inspire me.

xoxo
mama virg

About the Author

Virginia Nelson spends most days writing or plotting to take over the world. She hangs out with the greatest kids in history, plays in the mud and snow, drives far too fast, and sometimes screams at inanimate objects. Virginia likes knights in rusted and dinged up armor, heroes that snarl instead of croon, and heroines who can't remember to say the right thing even with an author writing their dialogue. She loves to hear from her readers and hopes you'll find her on social media.

Sign up for our Steals & Deals newsletter and be the first to hear about 99¢ releases from Virginia Nelson and other fantastic Entangled authors!

Reviews help other readers find books. We appreciate all reviews, whether positive or negative. Thank you for reading!

Her Temporary Hero
by Jennifer Apodaca

Wealthy, sexy, and emotionally haunted Logan Knight needs a temporary wife. Enter former beauty queen Becky Holmes. She and her baby are on the run from her dangerous ex and she'll do anything to protect her child...even agree to a sham marriage if it means protection. But Becky and her baby trigger Logan's darkest memories. While he tries to keep his distance, he can't. His attempt to have it all backfires into a betrayal that forces Becky into a heart-wrenching choice no woman should ever have to make.

The Tycoon's Socialite Bride
by Tracey Livesay

To avenge his mother's mistreatment at the hands of her upper-crust employer, selfmade real estate tycoon Marcus Pearson needs entree into their exclusive world. Enter D.C. socialite Pamela Harrington. Pamela will do anything to save her favorite cause, even agree to a marriage of convenience. She's sworn off powerful, driven men so she'll deny the way her pulse races with one look from Marcus's crystalline blue eyes. And he'll ignore the way his body throbs with each of her kisses. Because there's no way Marcus will lose his blue-collar heart to the blue-blooded beauty.

Printed in Great Britain
by Amazon